THE GIRL WHO
DREAMED ONLY GEESE

OTHER BOOKS BY
HOWARD NORMAN

FICTION

The Bird Artist
Kiss in the Hotel Joseph Conrad
The Northern Lights

FOLKLORE

Northern Tales
How Gloosekap Outwits the Ice Giants
Where the Chill Came From
The Wishing Bone Cycle

OTHER BOOKS ILLUSTRATED BY
LEO & DIANE DILLON

Her Stories
Many Thousand Gone
Northern Lullaby
Pish, Posh, Said Hieronymous Bosch
Aïda
The People Could Fly
Ashanti to Zulu
Why Mosquitoes Buzz in People's Ears

THE GIRL WHO DREAMED ONLY GEESE

and Other Tales of the Far North

Told by HOWARD NORMAN

Illustrated by LEO & DIANE DILLON

GULLIVER BOOKS

HARCOURT BRACE & COMPANY

San Diego   New York   London

Gulliver Books is a registered trademark of
Harcourt Brace & Company.

Library of Congress Cataloging-in-Publication Data
Norman, Howard A.
The girl who dreamed only geese, and other stories of the Far North/
told by Howard Norman; illustrated by Leo and Diane Dillon.
p.   cm.
"Gulliver Books."
Contents: The day puffins netted Hid-Well—Noah hunts a woolly mammoth—
Why the rude visitor was flung by walrus—
Uterisoq and the duckbill dolls—The wolverine's secret—
The girl who watched in the nighttime—The man who married a seagull—
Home among the giants—How the narwhal got its tusk—
The girl who dreamed only geese.
ISBN 0-15-230979-9
1. Inuit—Folklore.   2. Tales—Arctic regions.
[1. Inuit—Folklore.   2. Eskimos—Folklore.
3. Folklore—Arctic regions.]
I. Dillon, Leo, ill.   II. Dillon, Diane, ill.   III. Title.
E99.E7N63   1997
[398.2'089971]—dc20   96-20880

C E F D B

Printed in Singapore

CONTENTS

LAUGHTER IN THE KITCHEN

On November 3, 1979, I sat with Inuit storyteller Mark Nuqac in the kitchen of a mutual friend's house in Churchill, Manitoba. Over a period of six or seven hours, Mark Nuqac, then in his sixties, offered three renditions of the story "Noah and the Woolly Mammoths" in his native Qairnirmiut-Inuit dialect (which is largely spoken around Hudson Bay) and, for my further benefit, in hesitant yet eloquent English. There were the usual interruptions for meals, conversation, a walk to the post office, naps, but the day was dedicated to Mark Nuqac's recounting of the comic and tragic adventures of the Biblical Noah drifting into Hudson Bay on his ark.

Fifteen years later, as I review my notes, I am reminded that on November 3, 1979, it was snowing heavily. The tape recorder was situated amid coffee cups, doughnuts, and crayon drawings done by the household's five children, who ran in and out. The turn-of-the-century stove was cranked up, the smell of crisp bacon and lard thick in the air. The radio was playing softly in the bedroom, where Mark's aunt Mary was stitching up boots. North along the jigsaw coastline, polar bears were famished, restless for the freeze-up when they would meander out across the ice of Hudson Bay in search of seals. "Noah—he's my favorite to tell about," Mark said that same night. "When I was growing up, we had to go out, hunt food every day. Hunting, fishing, eh? Good luck, bad luck, *every day*. And now look, along comes this Noah fella, eh? His big boat-ark full of animals! He's got it pretty good!" There was a lot of laughter in the kitchen when he said that.

That day in November was not the first or last time Mark Nuqac shared this story with me. Between October 27, 1977, and October 10, 1980, he offered me fifteen renditions of "Noah and the Woolly Mammoths." I took each down by pencil, or tape recorder, in someone's kitchen, or in my room at the Beluga Hotel, in Churchill. None of his versions, of course, was perfectly identical to any other. The same essential chronology of events occurred, but the dialogues between characters, or the weather, or other details changed a little each time he told the story. Word by word, incident by incident, his Inuit story was constantly evolving, as Inuit stories have done for centuries. With his permission I have combined four of the Noah stories he deemed his best for this book. In dozens of hours working with all fifteen renditions, Mark Nuqac provided expert, unflagging, patient assistance; working with him was one of the most singular pleasures of my life.

Four other stories included here are the result of direct collaboration with two Inuit storytellers, Billy Nuuq and Moses Nuqac. Billy Nuuq and I first translated "Home among the Giants," "The Man Who Married a Seagull," and "The Girl Who Dreamed Only Geese" in Churchill, though our final working days together took place in a hospital and rest home in Montreal. Moses Nuqac and I translated "Why the Rude Visitor Was Flung by Walrus." A spry man in his eighties, with a round, deeply weathered face, he was as animated a raconteur as I have ever known. Though I did not know Moses as well as I did his nephew Mark, we sat at the same kitchen table—and a number of other tables in Churchill and two other villages—going through sheath after sheath of Moses's stories about shamans.

My retellings of the remaining five tales are the result of longtime correspondences between myself and linguists who have themselves worked closely for years with Inuit storytellers. Details of our collaborations can be found in the story notes at the back of this book.

In becoming part of the centuries-old tradition of bringing tribal stories to a wider audience, my most heartfelt ambition was to maintain the spirit, tone, and cultural integrity of the originals—for stories are not just about living things, they *are* living things, each with its own personal history.

In fact each of the ten tales in this collection could readily inspire a biography;

that is, the story *of* a story. Where was it first told? By whom? To which villages did it travel? Which persons told it best? How did it change over the centuries? And so on.

I hope that on first reading the ten folktales in *The Girl Who Dreamed Only Geese*, readers—whether children or adults—will experience the great joy of discovery, and that on rereading them, they will gain a sense of familiar anticipation as well.

The stories in *The Girl Who Dreamed Only Geese* were chosen because they entertain, educate, and place us inside the dramas of life in the harsh and beautiful Far North—from Siberia across Alaska and the Canadian Arctic to Greenland. I wanted to provide stories that allowed us to trek all the Northern landscapes: taiga, tundra, mountains, snow plains, fjords, iceberg-filled sea. Stories that let us eavesdrop on age-old conversations between people, animals, and spirits. Stories in which unpredictably wild, mischievous, slapstick funny, deadly serious, and just plain old day-to-day incidents all take place.

Perhaps most of all, I wanted to honor the request of six-year-old Mary Nuqac, who said, "Why not put together a bunch of stories and get really great pictures to go with them." So I thank the splendid Leo and Diane Dillon, whose art graces these pages, for fulfilling the second part of Mary Nuqac's request.

It is my conviction that Northern tales by turns solace and disturb us, provide indelible images and often unconventional wisdom, make us laugh, cry, and feel all the complicated emotions of being alive. In all these ways, they help us to clarify our world. And they quicken our imagination.

HOWARD NORMAN
Churchill, Manitoba
East Calais, Vermont

THE DAY
PUFFINS NETTED HID-WELL

I N A VILLAGE along the North Atlantic coast lived a man named Hid-Well. When he was a small boy, he had made himself a fine net by which to catch the stout, colorful birds called puffins. After many years of practice, he became a great hunter of puffins. Now he was an old man, but he still used his childhood net. Its weight and balance were as familiar to him as one of his own arms.

One summer morning Hid-Well's wife jostled him awake. "My mother, father, aunts, uncles, and cousins are on their way to our village," she said. "We must prepare a feast!"

This was big news. Hid-Well leapt from bed, threw on his clothes, and said, "As soon as I've had breakfast, I'll go to the sea and net puffins!"

He sat down for breakfast with his wife, daughter, and son. They all ate heartily. When the meal was over, Hid-Well took his net from its nail. "I'm on my way," he said. "I hope to bring back many puffins for supper."

"As you know, Father, I have long wanted to hunt puffins with you," the son said. "Why not take me along?"

"Not today," Hid-Well said firmly.

"The boy has learned from you how to hunt other animals," Hid-Well's wife said. "Someday he will need to bring home puffins for his own family."

"True," said Hid-Well, "but today I alone will provide puffins!"

"Good-bye, then, husband," Hid-Well's wife said. "Good luck in hunting."

"Yes, good luck," the daughter said.

Hid-Well turned to his daughter. "If your brother tries to follow me, hold him down until I'm out of sight. Stuff some dirt and pebbles into his mouth if need be. I don't want to hear him cry out."

Hid-Well set out for his puffin-netting place, a gather of high rocks and boulders near the sea. Only he knew its location. Not even his beloved wife knew this secret.

Now on this particular morning, Hid-Well had taken only a few steps from the village when he spun around. Just as he suspected, his son was close behind!

"I told you not to follow me!" Hid-Well said angrily. The boy crouched away, chortling like a wounded puffin.

"Oh, I hope that you won't mope around all day," Hid-Well said. "I can't respect anyone who does that. I won't ever go hunting with a moping boy."

"Father, listen. I can call in puffins as well as you can," the boy said.

The boy stood on a rock and let loose a shriek. "Aaaaauuueeeeiiiii!" Then he did it again and again and again. Hid-Well stepped back in awe. It was strange and won-

derful to see a boy so skillful at imitating a wild bird. For a moment Hid-Well simply stood there and marveled.

But then Hid-Well remembered how cross he was. In an instant he netted his son! He lifted the boy as high as the net would reach. "Father, let me go!" the boy cried out. "Let me go!" Finally, Hid-Well turned the net and out tumbled his son.

The daughter knew what to do now. She lassoed her brother's ankles with a sinew-rope, tripped him to the ground, then fell on top of him. Only his hands, feet, and howling mouth could be seen. "Stop crying out," she whispered strongly to him.

But the boy let fly a piercing call, so loud that the village sled dogs cowered and slunk away. Then, as her father had instructed, the daughter muffled his voice with dirt and pebbles. By the time he spit them out, Hid-Well could just barely be seen on the horizon.

The wind was at Hid-Well's back. He made good time. He carried only his net, a burlap sack, a small bundle of food, and his knife. He stopped only to drink from a stream or to nibble lard. He traveled through some lowland fog, then climbed up through the fog to a plateau where he felt sunshine on his face and hands. Mid-morning, as he neared the cliffs, he saw a few clouds roiling up darkly over the sea. *They are trying to bring in a storm,* he thought, *but they will not succeed.* And he was right, for by the time he reached his destination, the sky was perfectly clear. Throughout his many years of walking, Hid-Well had learned to pace himself. Still, when he sat a ways back from the cliff edge, he was panting. "Whew!" he said. "I'm weary. I had better rest before I start my climb." He lay on the ground and took a nap.

Soon he woke. He rubbed his eyes. He stretched and yawned. He took a deep breath. "Sun on my face—what a joyful feeling!" he said. "The sea smells like it did when I was a boy. And what's more, I have an afternoon of hunting puffins ahead of me. What a good life!"

He opened his bundle. He dipped his finger in the lard and savored its taste. When he had completely finished the lard, he started to climb. The loose rocks fell away in small avalanches. Near the top, he said, "Ah, here you are!" He ran his fingers over the highest boulders, familiar to him as the faces of his own wife and children. "Old friends, old friends. I am happy to be with you again."

Clutching his net tightly, he wedged himself between a flat, sharp, upright slab of rock and a boulder. He hid well. Wind whistled at his ears. He waited. He waited and waited. In his village he was admired for his patience. He stayed crouched there a long time. His legs cramped, his shoulders knotted, and even though he was expert at shading them from the sun, his eyes began to ache from staring hard out to sea. He had experienced exactly these hardships a thousand times before, and yet he was happy. "There is no place I'd rather be," he said. "And nothing I'd rather be doing."

He dozed awhile in the sun. The wind chafed his skin. He had just begun to dream of puffins when a hundred or more squalling voices startled him awake. "Puffins!" he cried with great joy. "Puffins!"

Now, over his lifetime, whenever a flock of puffins came in from the sea, steered by the wind, floating on updrafts, it looked to Hid-Well as if their numbers formed a wide net in the sky; it looked to him as if each bird were a knot in that net, and as if all of the knots were flying every which way. Hid-Well had studied puffins. He knew

that there was a better chance of drawing them close if you flattered them first. Puffins loved to be flattered and admired close-up. So Hid-Well shouted, "What a fine net you have made!"

Now a single puffin broke loose from the flock. Hid-Well saw his chance to entice it closer. He stood and waved his net. While the remainder of the flock held back, this adventurous one veered in toward Hid-Well and his net. But Hid-Well let it go! He wanted to catch more than one puffin at a time.

Now his plan was working. He was greatly amused to see the one puffin return to its parents, brothers, sisters, aunts, uncles, and cousins. Hid-Well cupped his ears, listening. You see, after so many years of hunting them, he knew the language of puffins. "Come on!" the young puffin said. "Come on!"

The flock drew nearer and nearer. Hid-Well was so excited, he could hear his own heart beating. "Get ready," he told himself. "Be alert."

So many puffins. So many!

Stretching his arms, waving his net, Hid-Well screeched, "Aaaaiiieee!"

The puffins careened past and Hid-Well held his ground. He felt wings brush past his hands, nick the top of his head, swirl at his knees. To be this close to puffins— what joy!

The flock swept off with a loud racket.

Now, usually, Hid-Well would have netted at least a few puffins. Yet this time was different; when he lowered his net and inspected it, there were no puffins to be found. The entire flock had eluded the net.

He was puzzled. "Bad luck, bad luck, bad luck," he said.

He rubbed a few cramps from his legs. He crouched down again. He shook his fist at the puffins, but he laughed at the same time. "They will be back," he said.

The wind had let up. It was quiet, the kind of quiet that arrives only after a flock of puffins has flown off.

Hid-Well looked to sea. He saw that the flock was coming full circle. Again he stood to his full height, waved his net, filled his lungs with brisk sea air, and let loose a wild yell, "Aaaaiiieee!"

But as the puffins gathered overhead, an astonishing thing took place. Hid-Well was swept up—the net of puffins scooped him right up into the sky. His own net dropped away. He struggled, somersaulted, and flailed away with his fists, but it was no use. He was captured. Of course he did not want to fall, but he did not want to stay up there, either.

"Let me go!" he pleaded. But in one great sweeping motion, the flock turned upside down, holding fast to Hid-Well. He grew dizzy and sick to his stomach.

Suspended by puffins high above the land, Hid-Well looked down to see an arctic fox loping on its way here or there. "Fox!" he called down. "Tell my family I'm a captive of puffins. Please—hurry!" But the fox didn't hear him. The fox didn't even glance up.

Now the puffins played blanket-toss with Hid-Well. They flipped him up into the air, catching him when he fell. This went on ten times. The puffins chattered, clicked, and chirred, "Tch, tch, tch"; they were delighted with this game!

Hid-Well bellowed, "Help! Help!" At first the high, harsh winds slapped back his words, but then the wind shifted and carried his voice all the way to his village. "Son, come rescue me! I'm in trouble!" Hid-Well was afraid the puffins would take him out to sea.

And indeed the puffins decided to do just that. They hauled Hid-Well far from shore. They hovered with him over the sea, on which he had paddled his kayak since he was a boy.

Now, back in his village, Hid-Well's son stepped from their house. He cupped his ears. He was puzzled. He thought that he had heard his father's voice, but his father was nowhere to be seen. The boy stood in the center of the village. He called his mother and sister to his side.

"What is it?" his mother asked. "What's the matter?"

"I believe I heard Father calling," the boy said. "He is in great danger."

They all tilted their heads, listening. But all they heard were the familiar sounds of village life. A frying pan clanked against an iron stove; two dogs yelped at each other; *plink, plink, plink*—some children flung stones against a tin shed roof with their slingshots. Hid-Well's family grew sad.

"I must try and find Father!" the boy said.

"Yes, go, hurry," his sister said.

The boy rushed about, stuffing a few items into a burlap sack, and then he set out. But in which direction should he travel—north, south, east, or west?

He walked in zigzag patterns across scrubby slopes, scrambled down dangerous ravines, poked along inlets, and inspected every cliff along the coastline, shouting as he went, "Father! Father!" He had no luck.

Near a cliff edge he felt desperate. "Maybe if I call in a puffin, it will tell me where my father is," he said. He tried to shriek, but his voice was hoarse, his throat raw from shouting. He could barely whisper. He reached into the burlap sack and pulled out an old crank-handled phonograph that many years before had washed up on shore after a storm. It was rusty. He cranked it up, and the needle scratched over the turntable, making a near-deafening screech. The boy kept cranking; the phonograph shrieked,

but no puffins appeared in the sky. Not one. He stood up, took a deep breath, and tried once again to make his own puffin-shriek, but still he could only rasp and croak. Sadly the boy went back home.

Meanwhile the puffins carried Hid-Well inland. They flew him over jagged rocks, then over deep, forbidding crevices. The wind tore at his clothes. Then, without warning, the puffins catapulted Hid-Well to the ground—just like that, they decided to let him go! In the hard fall, he broke all the bones in his feet. He landed next to his splintered net-handle. When he tried to stand, he let out a pained groan. "Oooh, oooh, my feet!" he said, and fell down again. For a long time he huddled there, moaning over his toes.

"I want to see my family!" he finally said.

He tore apart the burlap sack that had been belted to his waist and swaddled his feet in the strips he made. He discovered that the pole of his net was still strong enough to use as a crutch. He planted the pole on the ground, pulled himself up, and stood for a moment, trying to get his balance. His feet hurt badly. Still, he began to hobble toward home.

After many hours of difficult walking, Hid-Well drew close to his village. It was late in the day. His wife saw him and ran to him, shouting, "Husband, why are you limping so?"

When she embraced him, Hid-Well said, "I was netted by puffins."

She placed Hid-Well's arm over her shoulder and helped him walk to their house. There she immediately put him to bed. He pulled the blanket over his head. She sat next to the bed, packing his feet in ice.

9

Soon after, the doorway filled with the faces of Hid-Well's in-laws, aunts, uncles, and cousins.

"Hey, hey, let's sit down and roast up some puffins!" Hid-Well's father-in-law said. "Let's have a feast."

"There are no puffins," Hid-Well's wife said.

"Why not?" Hid-Well's father-in-law asked. "Hid-Well is supposed to be a great puffin hunter."

Hid-Well's wife pulled the blanket away. Everyone looked at Hid-Well. He was pale and shivering. He looked weak and besides that, he was ashamed.

"What happened to your husband?" Hid-Well's mother-in-law asked.

"He went out to net puffins," Hid-Well's wife said. "But the puffins netted him. They hovered him over the sea. Then they dropped him from a great height, which broke the bones of his feet. Now, as you can see, he's mending in bed. He told me the whole story."

"It's a hard story to believe," said Hid-Well's father-in-law. "In all of my years, I've seen how tricky puffins can be. I've even had a few dive at my head. But never, *never* have I heard of a man netted by puffins. It's a hard story to believe."

"Nonetheless, it is true," Hid-Well said from under his blanket.

Hid-Well's father-in-law led everyone to the empty cooking pot. They stared at it awhile. Hid-Well's father-in-law then took out a length of rope, dipped it in fish oil, and rubbed salt on it. "This is our supper," he said.

Hid-Well's father-in-law cut the rope into equal pieces. Hid-Well's in-laws, aunts,

uncles, cousins, wife, daughter, and son each took a single bite, and the rope was gone. They washed their meal down with cold water.

Then Hid-Well's father-in-law stepped into Hid-Well's room and said, "Rope is not delicious."

With no puffins to feast upon, everyone was very disappointed. The rope proved tough to digest. All of the relatives writhed on the ground, groaning; ahead of them lay a long night of bellyaches.

Through a hole in his blanket, Hid-Well saw this take place and felt worst of all. He was deeply ashamed. He wept.

Throughout the night, as his family and visitors tossed and turned in their sleep, Hid-Well repaired his net by lantern light. The next morning when everyone woke sore-boned and a little sick, Hid-Well said, "Forgive me for causing you a bad night. It's true that I'm hobbled by broken feet. But I'm going to feed all of you. I'm going to net puffins and won't come back until I've got enough for a feast."

Of course, right away his son said, "I want to go with you, Father. Aaaaiiieee!"

This time, Hid-Well said, "Yes, all right."

"Good luck in hunting," Hid-Well's wife said.

"Don't get netted by puffins!" his father-in-law said. Everyone fell laughing to the floor, except Hid-Well's wife, son, and daughter, and Hid-Well himself.

Hid-Well and his son set out, each carrying a net, each with a burlap sack belted to his waist. They traveled as fast as Hid-Well's broken feet would allow, which wasn't very fast at all. They stopped only once to drink from a stream and nibble bits of lard.

When they got to the boulders, Hid-Well spread his arms wide and said, "Look around you, son. All of these years, this place has been my secret."

"I'm happy to be here," Hid-Well's son said.

"Now I'm too weak to climb to my usual spot," Hid-Well said, pointing to the place he always hid. "You go up there. When you get to the highest boulders, hide well. Then make your very best puffin-shrieks."

"Yes, Father," the boy said.

The boy swiftly climbed up and hid. But he chose his own place, a few boulders away from where his father had pointed. He waited. He waited and waited, staring out to sea, shading his eyes from the sun.

Suddenly the boy pointed into the distance. "There!" he shouted. "Puffins!"

Down below, Hid-Well waved his net.

"Cram rocks into your pockets!" Hid-Well called up to his son. "If the puffins try to scoop you up, you'll be too heavy!"

The boy stuffed his parka with rocks. He stood to his full height and waved his net. "Aaaaiiieee! Aaaaiiieee! Aaaaiiieee!" he screeched.

Hid-Well looked at his son with great admiration. He was very proud.

Drawn by the boy's call, the puffins flew in and he netted six of them. The flock then dipped and rushed past Hid-Well, who nabbed ten!

The puffins flew off and roosted along the sheer cliff.

"Aaaaiiieee!" Hid-Well called.

"Aaaaiiieee!" his son answered.

The boy scrambled down to his father. "The wind chafed my face," he said. "What a joyful feeling!"

"Did your ankles get bruised against boulders?" Hid-Well asked.

"Yes, they did," the boy said. "And my hair is matted with puffin droppings and feathers. It is a fine day!"

12 They stuffed the puffins they had caught into the burlap sacks.

"Let's go home and feast on puffins," the boy said.

"Yes," said Hid-Well. "Between the two of us, we have plenty of puffins."

They traveled slowly but steadily toward the village. "Keep close track of the landmarks," Hid-Well said. "Someday you will need to find the boulders on your own."

Halfway home they stopped to rest. "I'm hungry. Let's build a fire and roast a puffin and eat it right here and now," the boy said.

"No, let's wait," Hid-Well said. "It's only right to divvy up the first puffin among my in-laws."

They sat awhile.

"Father, you have never lied to me," the boy said. "So I know that yesterday when you said you'd been netted by puffins, you told the truth. But why didn't the puffins grab *me* today? Why didn't they take *me* into the sky and hurl *me* down?"

"Well, some days there's good luck, some days bad," Hid-Well said. "One day puffins net a hunter, and the next they don't. It's a mystery. Whatever the reasons, that's simply how things go between people and puffins."

After they had rested, Hid-Well and his son continued home. There was a big welcome for them.

That night, Hid-Well, his wife, son, daughter, aunts, uncles, cousins, and in-laws sat around the fire and had a great feast.

The in-laws got to eat the first puffin. When everyone's stomach was full, Hid-Well's wife asked, "How was your day, husband?"

"It was a fine day," Hid-Well said. "Our son kept the net perfectly balanced. He made beautiful puffin-shrieks and caught six of these puffins himself!"

"And did the puffins lift you both into the sky?" Hid-Well's father-in-law asked, squinting his eyes and guffawing. All the cousins laughed; they taunted and teased Hid-Well. They still did not believe that he had been netted by puffins. But it did not matter, really. Hid-Well knew the truth and had helped provide a good meal as well. What's more, he had given his son the gift of his secret—the boulders where the puffins flew.

"Well, yes, the puffins might well have netted us today," Hid-Well's son said. "But they didn't. Maybe next time out we'll get netted by puffins! Who can tell?"

"Wife, daughter, you prepared these puffins with great care," Hid-Well said. "You flatter the puffins by doing so. Thank you. It was lucky that the puffins let us catch so many of them today and didn't carry my son and me out to sea or drop us in a ravine."

"Aaaaiiieee!" Hid-Well's son yelled.

After the meal, after much talking and laughing, Hid-Well hung his net on a nail. His son hung his own net on a nail. Everyone then went to sleep. In-laws, cousins, aunts, and uncles were scattered all over the house. In his bed Hid-Well felt better, though his feet would take a long time to mend. He was tired. Before he dozed off, he listened to familiar night-to-night village noises and was pleased.

NOAH HUNTS
A WOOLLY MAMMOTH

IN THE OLD, OLD DAYS, woolly mammoths were around. All up and down the coast of Hudson Bay, there were Inuit villages, and hunters from those villages would go right out into a blizzard and search for a woolly mammoth. Whenever a woolly mammoth was brought in, there was a big celebration and feast.

But the best hunters of woolly mammoths lived in a village known today as Eskimo Point.

Late one spring, flock after flock of arriving geese told the people of Eskimo Point of a great flood far to the south. "As we left on our travels, we saw the ground covered with water," the geese said. "Only one family of human beings survived. They had a big boat. One pair of each kind of animal got on the boat, too."

The villagers listened closely. They believed the geese. The geese often told them of strange goings-on far to the south. The people of this village were always curious and enjoyed hearing such stories.

"In which direction was this big boat traveling?" the eldest hunter in the village asked the geese.

"North," the geese said.

That autumn, when the last of the geese flew south, a few hunters from Eskimo Point were standing on some boulders, scanning the sea, talking about the weather. Suddenly one hunter called out, "Look!"

They all saw an enormous boat floating out in Hudson Bay. They had never before seen such a boat. They lived in a time of kayaks. So when the hunters saw this boat, they were afraid, but curious as well.

"What should we do?" they asked the eldest hunter.

"Let's take a closer look," he said.

They got into their kayaks and paddled out. When they drew near to the boat, the eldest hunter paddled right up and touched it. "This boat is made of wood!" he said.

Now, there was not much wood in the old-time villages. Sometimes after spring thaw, pieces of driftwood washed up on shore, but that was a rare occurrence.

Along the side of the boat, just below deck, were square windows. Suddenly all sorts of strange creatures appeared in the windows—such striped, spotted, colorful creatures as the hunters had never seen! They gawked.

"What kinds of animals are those?" one hunter asked.

"I don't know," the eldest hunter said. "But, look. Some of them have a lot of meat on their legs, shoulders, rumps, and backs. Maybe we can eat one or two."

Just then, a bearded man in a white, flowing robe appeared on deck.

"My name is Noah," he said.

"What kind of boat is this?" the eldest hunter asked.

"It's called an ark," Noah said. "It was made to carry animals from here to there on the sea."

"How do you paddle such a big boat?" the eldest hunter asked.

"It just drifts with the wind," Noah answered.

"What you see us paddling are kayaks," the eldest hunter said. "When we kill a seal, we carry it home across the bow of a kayak. When we catch fish, we haul them home in our kayaks. But kayaks aren't big enough to keep live animals in. It's a good idea, though, if a boat is as big as yours."

"Where is your family?" another hunter asked Noah.

"Below deck," Noah said.

"Let us see them," the eldest hunter said.

"Wife, son, daughter," Noah called down.

Soon Noah stood with his family on deck. His wife, son, and daughter wore white robes just like Noah's.

"Why did you come here?" the eldest hunter asked.

"We had no choice," Noah said. "There was a great flood. It drowned our homeland. It rained for forty days and forty nights."

"Well, we've had blizzards that lasted that long," the eldest hunter said.

"Yes, we had some bad luck," Noah said.

"Still, you're lucky to be traveling with so many animals you can eat," said the eldest hunter. "Up here, we have to work hard every day to catch animals. If we don't go out every day to hunt, our families might starve. By the way, are there any seals on your ark?"

"No," said Noah.

"Any beluga whales?" the eldest hunter asked.

20   "No," said Noah.

"Well, if you share some of the animals you have on the ark with us, we will provide you with fish, seal meat, and maybe even some woolly mammoth meat, if we catch a woolly mammoth, which is a difficult thing to do."

"I can't do that," Noah said. "I'm saving these animals. I'm going to make my way back south and let them go."

The eldest hunter turned to his companions. "This man Noah will not share his good luck in traveling with so many fat animals," he said. "So be it."

Although he was angered by Noah's selfishness, the eldest hunter said, "Still, let's leave Noah and his family some fish!" The hunters tossed a lot of fish onto the deck of the ark. One hunter threw Noah a spear, too.

"Maybe you'll figure out how to use that spear," the eldest hunter said. "Let me warn you of something. It's getting close to winter. Soon the great blizzards will arrive. Your ark will be locked in ice. Deep into winter, those animals on board your ark will come in handy."

"I'll catch fish through the ice to feed my family," Noah said. "And I have plenty of hay for the animals." Noah held out some hay in his fist, for the Inuit villagers had never before seen hay.

The hunters paddled back to shore.

For the remainder of the autumn, Noah managed to provide fish for his family. Curious about the ark, villagers now and then stood on boulders to look at it. Once in a while a villager would say, "Again today, crosswinds wouldn't let the ark leave the bay." But mostly they had little time for Noah and his family. They had to prepare for winter.

The brief autumn ended. The first blizzards of winter swirled in hard and fast. Just as the eldest hunter had warned, the ark was locked in ice. Villagers stood on boulders, gazing across the sea ice.

One day in the heart of winter, there was a great uproar in the village because a woolly mammoth had been sighted down near the frozen sea! A mammoth is a powerful beast, with shaggy hair, curved tusks, and eyes high up off the ground. It was a dangerous task to hunt a woolly mammoth, but that's just what the old-time hunters did, for a woolly mammoth could feed an entire village for many days.

Hearing that a woolly mammoth had been sighted, the village hunters immediately set out after it. They found the woolly mammoth tusking up snow in order to get to the grasses. As the hunters closed in on the woolly mammoth, the wind shifted and the mammoth caught the scent of the men. It fled out on the ice toward the ark. The hunters followed and when the woolly mammoth got to the ark, it pierced its tusks into the top part of the hull, then hoisted itself on deck. Now there were gaping holes in the ark. Using seal fat, the hunters quickly caulked up the holes.

"Noah!" the eldest hunter called up. "See how we have mended your ark! Now, in exchange for our help, let us have that woolly mammoth!"

"No!" Noah called down. "It hauled up on my boat, so it's mine! I'll kill it, roast it, and my family will have a feast!"

"There's plenty to go around," the eldest hunter said. "Toss down a shoulder, at least."

"No!" said Noah.

The hunters watched as Noah hurled his spear at the woolly mammoth. But he missed!

Now, woolly mammoths hate to be hunted so clumsily, and this one lost its temper! It went wild, thrashing about, flinging planks of wood out on the sea ice. The hunters gathered up the splintered planks.

"It is one thing to have a piece of wood drift to shore," the eldest hunter said. "But it is quite another to have wood flung out to us by a woolly mammoth! What good luck!"

On deck, the woolly mammoth roared and reared up, swinging its shaggy head back and forth.

Noah picked up his spear and was just ready to throw it again, when the beast started toward him. Suddenly it hit a patch of ice, slipped, crashed down, and died.

"You see, there!" Noah boasted. "What a good hunter I am!"

But the hunters knew that Noah had not really had good luck in hunting; the woolly mammoth had just had bad luck in falling to its death.

"Well, now that the woolly mammoth is dead," the eldest hunter said, "it is customary to share your good fortune. Why not at least give us a shoulder or leg—you can keep the rest."

"No!" said Noah. "The woolly mammoth was on my ark when it died, so I will keep it!"

The hunters were angered and disappointed. "He won't offer us a morsel of woolly mammoth!" one hunter said. "This is a day of unusual sadness."

The hunters returned to their village and called a meeting. Everyone in the village—grandmothers, grandfathers, mothers, fathers, children, babies—gathered by a bonfire made from planks of the ark.

The eldest hunter stepped forth. "This visitor—Noah—clearly doesn't know how to behave," he said.

"What should we do about it?" a woman asked.

"Noah and his family will not be welcome in our village," the eldest hunter said. "When they need food later, let's just leave scraps of fish halfway between our village and the ark, out on the sea ice."

In ten days' time, scraps of fish were left out on the sea ice for Noah and his family. The villagers saw Noah's son and daughter fetch them back to the ark. "Just as I thought," said the eldest hunter, "they have already run out of woolly mammoth."

It was even colder now, and the blizzards were more frequent and stronger than ever. Still, the villagers stayed warm by the heat of seal-oil lamps, whereas Noah and his family shivered. They stuffed straw under their robes. They were flea-bitten. The villagers had fish, seal, and ptarmigan to eat. Noah and his family had had five feasts of woolly mammoth in a row, but now they were reduced to nibbling straw dipped in lard. They hadn't known enough to store food for a later time. They had skidded the tusks across the ice—they hadn't hung them out to thank the spirit of the woolly mammoth, the one who fell to its death. Noah didn't know how to chisel holes in the ice to catch fish. He didn't even own an ice chisel. And just as the eldest hunter had predicted, in their hunger Noah and his family turned to eating the strange animals, one by one. However, they did not eat all of the animals on the ark. One night some villagers watched as a number of strange animals escaped out over the ice, disappearing into the distance, heading south.

Now it happened that on a day of particularly fierce crosswinds, Noah stumbled toward Eskimo Point. This was not nearly as exciting as when a woolly mammoth was sighted, but still it was interesting, and the people gathered around Noah, who stood shivering in the middle of their village.

"My family is starving," Noah said. "We'd like some food to eat."

Villagers tossed Noah a few scraps of fish and a thumb-size piece of lard. Then they poked him with spears. They didn't poke into him, only pushed him out of the village. Poking, poking, poking, they escorted Noah back across the ice to his ark.

The very next day a woolly mammoth was sighted, and the hunters harnessed their dogs and took sleds out after it. Same as before, the woolly mammoth caught the human scent and made its way out to the ark. It hoisted itself on deck. Noah picked up his spear.

The hunters stood on the ice near the ark. "Let me teach you the proper song to lull the woolly mammoth closer," the eldest hunter called up to Noah. "I've lulled woolly mammoths many times in my life. I can do it in the proper fashion. I will teach you!"

"No!" said Noah. "I'll sing the woolly close."

Noah began to sing, but his singing was awful, and it enraged the woolly mammoth, which lowered its head and went at Noah with its tusks.

Noah reared back his arm and hurled the spear. The spear wobbled in the air past the woolly's head and landed out on the ice.

The eldest hunter threw Noah's spear back to him.

"There's a proper way to kill a woolly mammoth," the eldest hunter said. "Noah, let me teach you, and you can share the woolly mammoth with us. If you hunt the woolly mammoth improperly, you will insult it, and it will tear apart your ark and kill you and your family. A woolly mammoth can do that."

But Noah was stubborn. "No! No! No!" he cried. He picked up his spear and flung it at the woolly mammoth again, and again he missed!

"From that close up, it is very hard to miss a woolly mammoth entirely," the eldest hunter said, and the other hunters laughed loudly.

But then the woolly mammoth spoke in human words.

"I am leaving the top of the world!" the woolly mammoth said. "All of the other mammoths are going to leave as well. We are digging through the ice, and we are going under the ground to live. We are insulted by a wobble-speared hunter for the last time!"

With this, the woolly mammoth rolled itself off the ark, and when it hit the sea ice, it stood up and ran off to shore. There it disappeared into a crevice in the ground.

"Look, there!" the eldest hunter said. "And there! And over there!"

All along the coastline, the hunters saw woolly mammoths disappearing into the ground.

"Now they are gone," the eldest hunter said. "We won't hunt woolly mammoths again."

The hunters went sadly home and that night in the village, the last of the planks from the ark were lit and a meeting was held by the fire. Again everyone was there.

"This Noah," said the eldest hunter, "is hopeless. He can't live up here in winter. He can't hunt in blizzards. He is too stubborn to learn. Now he has insulted away the mammoths. There is only one thing to do. We must invite his family to spend the rest of the winter with us. We can't stand by and watch people starve out on the ice. When the spring ice-breakup comes, we will send them on their way!"

One hunter went out and fetched Noah and his family. The villagers built them a hut at the very outskirts of the village. They weren't invited into anyone's house for a meal, for gossip, or for a drum-dance. They were shunned. But they were given

warm blankets and seal-oil lamps, and every morning scraps of fish, seal, and ptarmigan were left in clear sight of their hut.

One day late in the following spring when the geese returned, some hunters went out to talk to them. "The floodwaters have soaked back into the earth, far to the south," the geese said.

The hunters listened carefully and believed the geese. They went back to the village and told this news to the eldest hunter. He walked directly over to Noah's hut.

"Noah," the eldest hunter said, "it's time for you to leave our village. You must leave the ark behind and walk south along the coast. Here is a bundle of food."

The villagers gathered and watched Noah and his family set out on foot, heading south.

When they were out of sight, the ark was broken up for firewood, which it provided all summer and well into the heart of the next winter. Grievous to say, the woolly mammoths kept their promise and never again were seen on the top of the world.

WHY THE RUDE VISITOR WAS FLUNG BY WALRUS

I N AN INUIT VILLAGE there lived a great wizard—a shaman. Every so often he would turn into a walrus, swim out to Walrus Island, haul himself up by his tusks, and wedge in with the herd, all basking, grunting, lolling about in the sun. At day's end he would swim back to shore, become a man again, walk into his house, and say to his family, "It was pleasant to be amid walrus. They told me much gossip. I hunted near the sea bottom. I nodded, rolled my lardy neck back and forth in the air, and sharpened my tusks on a rock. All in all, a fine day." And even though he was a man again, he would smell like a walrus for a few days, so everyone knew where he had been.

On a pleasant, sunny day during the spring ice-breakup, the old shaman was sitting outside with his family. He was combing out his sled dogs. His son was mending a harness. His daughter and wife were cleaning fish. In the distance icebergs calved off with great, thundering roars.

"I think I'll make a visit to the walrus soon," the old man said.

"After we are done working here," his wife said, "let's go to the sea edge and watch the icebergs calving."

The old man finished combing out his dogs. The boy held up the newly mended harness. The fish were all cleaned and laid out.

"Let's go to the sea now!" the daughter said. Everyone was happy.

But just as they were about to set out, a trusted friend ran up. He had a worried, fearful look on his face and was panting hard.

"Catch your breath," said the old man. "We will stand with you until you're ready to speak."

When the friend calmed down, the old man said, "Now, friend, what is the matter?"

"A not-invited man is at the edge of our village!" the friend said. "He just suddenly showed up! He is wearing a smelly shirt and necklaces of tusks. He has tusks braided up in his hair, too. He looks like a menace. He says he is a great, great wizard—far greater than you! He is here to challenge you!"

Now, the old man loved three things most in the world: He loved to sit working with his family. He loved to become a walrus and gossip with walrus. And he loved to stand at the sea edge and watch the ice-breakup.

"I am annoyed," the old man said. "A not-invited man is interrupting my day!"

"You must meet with him," the old man's wife said.

"We'll all go with you, Father," his son said.

They walked to the edge of the village. Sure enough, there was a not-invited man, all festooned in tusks. He was spitting and growling fiercely. He was clacking his tusks. He was waving a narwhal tusk back and forth in the air. He stabbed at some villagers who had come too close to him—the villagers gasped and stepped back. He had lice jumping out of his hair. He had matted knots of bird feathers braided down his back.

By now the entire village had gathered. The old man stepped up to the not-invited man.

"Those are nice tusks," the old man said. "You spit nicely, too. What's more, your lice are bigger than any I've ever seen in all my years. Now that I've seen your ferociousness close-up—leave our village at once!"

"I'm here to challenge you!" the not-invited man said. "I'm a far more powerful magician than you!"

"You smell worse than a rotting whale carcass!" the old man said.

"What?" said the not-invited guest. "Did I hear you insult me?"

"You smell worse than a boot that has been vomited into by everyone in my village," said the old man.

"What?" said the not-invited man, waving the tusk. "How dare you!"

"You are only fit to live in a polar bear's anus," said the old man.

Angry, angry, the not-invited man tore at his hair, growling. Then he said, "I will show you one of my tricks."

The not-invited man slid the narwhal tusk straight through his cheeks and left it protruding from each side of his face so that everyone could see.

"There's no blood coming out!" one villager cried. "This is truly powerful magic!"

The not-invited man twisted the tusk from his cheek and flung it at the feet of the old man. "Now, old man," the not-invited man said, "*you* leave this village! I am the shaman here from now on!"

"Well, what you did with the narwhal tusk was a sleight of hand, all right," the old man said. "But you aren't a true shaman. You're only a small-time magician who stinks worse than a glob of seagull intestines! I'll tell you what. I'll let you scrub your shirt at our sea edge. Then you can dry it out by our fire. Then you leave behind all of

those tusks, plus that narwhal tusk—that's my bargain. If you agree to it, I promise not to harm you. I'll let you go."

"Your threats don't frighten me!" the not-invited man said. "I'm the shaman here now!"

"No, you're not," said the old man.

"I am!" the not-invited guest said, spitting.

"No!" said the old man.

Angry, angry, angry, the not-invited guest took off his smelly shirt and pushed it into the old man's face. With this, the old man leapt on the not-invited guest! They tore at each other. Their faces were contorted, as if seen through ice. Their mouths frothed up. They gouged each other's eyes. They locked arms and legs. Their bones cracked. They spit, snarled, grunted.

"My husband is winning!" the old man's wife shouted.

"No—the other man is winning!" said a villager.

"No—the old man is winning!" another villager said.

"No, no, no—," others said, but the wrestling match was so fierce, no one could actually tell who was winning.

The battle went on into the night. The old man's family built a fire. The two men wrestled near the fire. All night, all night, the wrestling continued. Snarling. Biting. Scratching. No villager slept. Everyone was watching.

Early the next morning, the wrestlers backed away from each other. But nothing had been decided.

The old man went to the sea edge. "Look, there!" he said. "The icebergs are almost through calving! If I have to keep wrestling to prove myself, I'll miss the entire ice-breakup. I'm annoyed."

When the old man turned to go back to his village, he saw the not-invited man directly behind him. All the villagers were there, too.

"Watch this," the not-invited man said.

The not-invited man got into a kayak. He swiftly paddled through flat and jagged floes of ice, out to Walrus Island. There he climbed on top of a gather of walrus. Immediately, the walrus flung him from one side of the island to the other; tusks to tusks he was flung, tusks to tusks. All day—all day. Then all through the night, the not-invited man was flung by walrus. Finally, the next morning, the not-invited man paddled the kayak back to the mainland. He stood in the middle of the village and shouted, "There! You see! Out on Walrus Island I flew! Only a true shaman can fly!"

"No! Don't fool yourself!" the old man said. "You weren't flying—you were being walrus-flung is all."

The not-invited man looked around. "Hey," he said, "I like the middle of the village. I'll build my hut here!"

And he did. The not-invited man built a hut right in the middle of the village.

"You'd better swim down to the Land-of-the-Dead and ask advice of your ancestors," the old man's wife said to the old man. "Things have gone far enough."

"You're right, wife," the old man said.

You see, whenever bad, bad luck struck the village, the old man swam down to the Land-of-the-Dead. Wise ancestors dwelled there. The old man was always welcome, for he was a great wizard, but anyone else who tried to dive that deep in the sea would drown.

The old man called together his wife, his son, and his daughter. "Son," he said, "be hospitable to our guest. Take him whaling."

"All right, Father," the son said.

"Daughter," the old man said, "be hospitable to our guest. Sew together a blanket."

"Wife," the old man said, "be hospitable to our guest. Invent a recipe especially for him."

"All right, husband," his wife said.

"Good-bye, family," the old man said.

"Good-bye, good-bye, good-bye," his family replied.

The old man walked to the village edge, took a deep breath, smelled the walrus out on Walrus Island, took another deep breath, and inhaled the smell of the rancid shirt of the not-invited guest, then leapt into the sea and dove to the Land-of-the-Dead.

The village of his ancestors at the bottom of the sea was tidy. Everything was in order. The old man went directly to the house of his grandfather and grandmother. But they were not at home. The old man went to a nearby house; it was a house in which three of his elder cousins dwelled—each had had his kayak capsized by walrus and had drowned. "Where are my grandmother and grandfather?" the old man said.

"They swam up to the surface to watch the ice-breakup," his cousins told him. "You know how much they love to see the ice-breakup."

"Yes," said the old man.

"Why are you here?" one cousin asked.

"I need advice," the old man said.

"We'll give you advice," another cousin said.

"No," said the old man, "I don't want cousin-advice."

"Well, your uncles live close by. How about them?" a cousin asked.

"No, I don't want uncle-advice," the old man said.

"You've got some aunts down here, too," a cousin said.

"Yes, sometimes aunt-advice is good," the old man said. "But I don't want it this time."

"All right," said a cousin, "wait for your grandparents, then."

"Good-bye, then," the old man said. He went back to his grandmother and grandfather's house and waited on a bench.

Back up on the surface of the world, in the old man's village, the not-invited man was ornery. He stomped about, crying out, "I'm hungry! Get me something to eat! If I don't get something to eat soon, I'll fold up my shirt and send it up somebody's nostrils! I'll turn the sled dogs inside out! I'll cause you no end of troubles!"

"We believe you, rude guest," the old man's son said. "Let me take you whaling. We'll try and catch a whale for you to eat."

"Let's go," said the not-invited guest.

The old man's son and the rude not-invited man walked to the sea. "Look!" the old man's son said. "Follow that blowhole spray. You'll find a whale. Call down to it, 'Whale—let me have a look at you!' The whale will rise to the top of the sea. Then you can catch it."

The not-invited man paddled a kayak out. He followed the drifts of blowhole spray. He paddled fast and caught up with the whale. "Whale—let me have a look at you!" he called down.

The whale rushed to the surface. But instead of letting the rude not-invited man kill it, the whale flipped its tail and hurled him to Walrus Island! There the man was flung by walrus, tusks to tusks, back and forth across the island. Finally the walrus let him go and he swam back to the mainland.

The rude man stomped into the village. "I was betrayed!" he hollered. "Now I'm going to fold my shirt and send it up somebody's nostrils!"

"Oh, don't be angry!" the old man's daughter said. "Look, I've built a fire. Hang your shirt near it to dry out. Sit here with me. I've sewn a blanket for you."

She handed him the blanket. But while the not-invited man was out chasing blowhole spray with her brother, she had hidden seal bladders inside the hem.

The not-invited man hung his shirt by the fire. He lay down under the blanket. Worn out from being flung by walrus, he fell right asleep. As he slept, the daughter wrapped the blanket around him tightly, sewed it shut with gut thread, dragged him to the sea edge, inflated the seal bladders, and rolled the not-invited man into the sea. The winds drifted him out to Walrus Island. There, a walrus scooped him up and flung him across the island. Tusks to tusks, tusks to tusks, tusks to tusks, he was flung. This woke him up!

Finally the walrus let him go and he swam back to the mainland. He was furious! He stomped into the village again. "I'm going to turn the sled dogs inside out!" he shouted.

"Oh, oh, oh—don't do that just yet," the old man's wife said. "Remember, you haven't had a meal yet. To turn dogs inside out, you'll need strength. Sit down. I'll feed you."

The not-invited man sat down. The old man's wife brought out a cauldron of broth. She ladled out some broth into a bowl and handed it to the not-invited man. He sipped it. He took another sip. Then he clutched his stomach and began to groan. "You have poisoned me!" he cried out. "What was in that broth?"

"It is a special recipe," the old man's wife said. She stuck the ladle into the cauldron and pulled out the not-invited man's smelly shirt. "Isn't it delicious!" she said.

The not-invited man writhed on the ground, groaning. Just then the old man flew up from the sea and landed in the village.

The old man looked at the not-invited man.

"What is the matter here?" he asked. "Has my family not shown you hospitality?"

"Things are not going as I want them to," the not-invited man moaned.

The old man turned to the gathered villagers.

"I have been down to the Land-of-the-Dead," he said. "It was a good visit. I asked for advice from my grandparents. I got advice."

Having said that, the man magically spun out a length of seal rope strong enough to hold the weight of a man. He quickly knotted it around the not-invited man. He then lifted himself right into the air, dangling the rude visitor beneath him! He hovered the visitor for everyone to see. Then he flew out to Walrus Island. He dropped the not-invited man down to the walrus.

Immediately the walrus began to fling the visitor.

All day—all day, the visitor was walrus-flung. Now and then many walrus would tumble into the sea to hunt. But there were always enough walrus left on the island to fling the visitor!

So, finally, life in the village was calm again. The old man sat with his family. He worked on a new dog harness. His wife scrubbed out the cauldron. His son repaired the kayak. His daughter combed out the dogs.

"It is unfortunate that you had to miss some of the ice-breakup this year," the old man's daughter said.

"Yes," said the old man. "But it was good to see my grandparents again, and they were kind to ask the walrus to fling the not-invited man for twenty days!"

When the dog harness was properly made, the cauldron scrubbed clean, the kayak mended, and the dogs combed out, the daughter said, "Look what I've made." She had fashioned the uncooked scraps of the not-invited man's shirt into a doll. She tossed it to the dogs, who snarled at it, gnawed at it, and tossed it about.

The family went to the sea edge. They looked out to Walrus Island.

"That man is visiting all parts of the island," the old man's wife said.

"Yes, but he is not flying on his own," the old man said.

UTERITSOQ AND
THE DUCKBILL DOLLS

WHO HAD THE REPUTATION for being the most stubborn man in all of the coastal villages of Greenland? It was a man named Uteritsoq. No one could be as obstinate as he. His own wife called him Stubborn as a nickname.

Uteritsoq was a good provider, though. He brought in fish, seals, and walrus for his family and his village. He stubbornly paddled his kayak through choppy seas out to the walrus-hunting grounds. There he would stubbornly wait for the walrus to show, even if hail whipped his face, even if he had to tuck himself between rocks out of the wind for days in a row. When the walrus showed up, Uteritsoq had a talent for picking the most stubborn one. He'd fight it. Then he'd cut up the walrus, back, fins, all of it, and haul it home by himself. He didn't want anyone's help.

Now it happened that Uteritsoq had a beautiful wife. But she was very unhappy. She had wanted a child so badly, and just a few days earlier she had lost a child before it had lived even a day! There was great sadness throughout the village.

45

Crying, weeping, sobbing. Uteritsoq's wife went into mourning. One by one the other women in the village came to her house to sit and weep with her. According to traditional rules, she was not to do work of any sort—no sewing, no fish cleaning, no mending, no cooking. Nothing. Mourning was enough work. Weeping was enough work. Dreaming about the lost child was enough work.

However, Uteritsoq felt crowded by the weeping in his house. He watched his wife's quaking shoulders, her tears, how she tore at her hair, her constant frown—it all made Uteritsoq restless and confused. He wanted to flee from his own house. So he did.

It was a bright, clear day. "I'll go out and hunt walrus," he said. He went out behind the back of his house to get his kayak. Yet when he looked closely, he saw that the skin of his kayak was torn. He couldn't paddle out to sea with the kayak in such condition; water would leak in and he would sink to the bottom. He walked back to his house and said, "Wife, you must mend the skin of my kayak!"

There were four other women sitting with his wife.

"Husband, you well know I'm forbidden to do any kind of work just now," Uteritsoq's wife said.

But stubborn Uteritsoq said, "Drag my kayak to the edge of the sea and mend it!"

"Listen to you!" his wife said. "You are like a barking dog. Go away, dog! I will not do any work during my time of mourning."

"You will mend my kayak!" Uteritsoq said.

46   "No!" said his wife.

"No! No! No! No!" said the other women. They leapt on Uteritsoq and pummeled him with their fists. But he threw them off and scattered them outside.

"Be gone!" he called after them. "This is my house! This is the house of Uteritsoq!"

Then he turned to his wife. "Mend my kayak!" he shouted.

"No!" his wife said.

But Uteritsoq sat cross-legged in front of her and began to chant, "Mend my kayak! Mend my kayak! Mend my kayak!" using his worst, most gravelly singing voice. He chanted all night. His wife got no sleep whatsoever.

In the morning Uteritsoq said over and over again, "Drag my kayak to the sea and mend it!"

Finally his wife could stand it no longer. She put her hands over her ears and cried, "All right—I'll mend the kayak! But then paddle off and leave me alone for some days with my sorrow."

All the villagers gathered. They said, "Poor, poor woman," as they watched her drag the kayak to the sea edge. There she took out her gut thread and bone needle and began to stitch the kayak. But right away, the sewing thread began to hum loudly! The humming grew louder and louder.

"Stop!" cried Uteritsoq, who was standing close by.

But his wife was too caught up in her sewing and stitched even faster. Now the humming became an awful muttering. The muttering grew louder! It became a barking sound.

Frightened, Uteritsoq's wife flung the needle and thread into the sea! When the needle and thread hit the water, they turned into a giant dog, its snarling lips pulled back, its teeth chattering. The dog leapt to shore and stood directly in front of Uteritsoq's wife.

"Why do you stitch-mend a kayak while you are in mourning?" the giant dog asked. "You know full well it is forbidden!"

"My husband is Uteritsoq," she said.

"Oh, the stubborn one," the dog said.

"Yes," said Uteritsoq's wife. "That's him, standing right there."

"He is too stubborn for me to handle," the dog said. "I'll fetch my master, Moon Man, to take care of this."

The dog flew up to the moon and returned with its master, Moon Man, who was riding a sled.

Now, whenever a woman broke the taboo and did any sort of work during her time of mourning, Moon Man or his dog flew down to berate her and to warn her that if she did it again, Moon Man might bring down wild, whistling winds such as are only found on the moon, and he would careen those winds every which way, tumbling dogs, houses, sleds into the sea. He would punish the whole village!

But this time was different. Moon Man said, "Uteritsoq, it was stupid of you to make your wife mend your kayak while she was in mourning! I watched the whole thing from the moon. You forced her to break one of the oldest rules!"

Uteritsoq did not like to be told he was wrong, so he leapt on Moon Man and began to choke him. Uteritsoq clenched Moon Man's neck tighter and tighter.

"Uteritsoq," Moon Man struggled to say, "you know that I control the tides. If you work my death, there will be no more ebb tide or flood tide. Seals and walrus will no longer be able to swim up to the rocky beaches. Your people will no longer be able to hunt them!"

"So be it!" Uteritsoq said, throttling Moon Man all the harder.

"If you work my death," said Moon Man, who was just about to black out, "it will cause an eclipse for all time!"

Hearing this, Uteritsoq suddenly released his grip and let Moon Man go. Uteritsoq could not bear the idea of living in ceaseless dark.

Moon Man got to his feet. He harnessed his dog and levitated his dogsled into the air. "I'm returning to the moon," Moon Man said. "It would be good for you to follow me. If you dare to fly, you will see sights you have never before seen."

Uteritsoq took this as a challenge. "All right," he said, "give me some magic, then."

Moon Man flung down his magic whip.

"Snap this whip above the rumps of your dogs," Moon Man said. "The dogs will be able to fly you to the moon."

Uteritsoq picked up the whip. He snapped it a few times in the air.

"I offer you a warning, though," Moon Man said. "Up on the moon, if you happen upon a high rock, take great care to drive your sled behind it. Do not pass it on the sunny side. For if you do, you will lose your stomach guts!"

"Ha, ha, ha!" Uteritsoq laughed, for he thought that Moon Man was only trying to frighten him. "I'm not afraid."

"Very well, then," said Moon Man. "I'll see you up on the moon."

Uteritsoq went to his house. His wife was there.

"Trying to throttle Moon Man was pretty stupid," she said.

"I'm flying to the moon now," Uteritsoq replied.

"Good," she said. "I'll be in our house, mourning."

"So be it," said Uteritsoq.

"Good-bye, husband," she said.

"Good-bye, wife," he said.

Uteritsoq harnessed his dogs to his sled, cracked the whip over their rumps, and immediately flew toward the moon. The magic worked. It did not take long. When

he landed on the moon, Uteritsoq said, "Get, get, get!" to his dogs and started over the terrain. Quite soon Uteritsoq came to a high rock. The long path behind it was dark, but the path on the sunny side looked short. "I'm in a hurry to get to Moon Man, to see sights I've never seen before," he said out loud. "Why should I take the dark side when the sunny side is a shortcut?"

He started around the sunny side, and when he drew close to the rock, he heard a woman singing a drum-song and whetting her knife. Even when she noticed Uteritsoq, she kept on singing, and he could hear how the steel of her knife hummed. What startled Uteritsoq was that this woman whet her knife on her own knees!

"I am powerful—don't come near me!" the woman said.

"I'm not afraid of you," Uteritsoq replied. And having said as much, he called, "Get, get, get!" to his dogs and tried to trample the woman under his sled. The woman stood up—up and up, until she was a giant. She flicked Uteritsoq with her finger, and he was slammed against a rock and knocked out cold.

When Uteritsoq came to, he was cradled in the lap of Moon Man. "You were stupid to try and trample that woman," Moon Man said. "She's the strongest of the spirits up here. You were too stubborn to heed my warning."

"Hey, what's that hollow feeling I have in my stomach?" Uteritsoq cried.

"Well, that woman pulled out your stomach guts!" Moon Man said. "But she took pity on you and left me with some magic stones."

Moon Man set out the stones.

"What can these stones do?" Uteritsoq asked.

Moon Man picked up one stone, handed it to Uteritsoq, and said, "Look through this stone and scan the terrain."

Uteritsoq looked through the stone. He looked all around him, out into the distance. Suddenly he shouted, "I see my stomach guts! They are over by some rocks—over there!"

"Well, go fetch them, then!" Moon Man said.

Uteritsoq went to the rocks, then carried his guts back.

"Now, lie down on your back," Moon Man said. "I'll place another stone on your stomach."

Uteritsoq lay on his back. Moon Man set a stone on his stomach. He pushed Uteritsoq's guts through the magic stone, right back into his body.

"There," said Moon Man, "look down over the edge of the moon through this stone."

Moon Man handed Uteritsoq yet another stone. Uteritsoq peered through it.

"Don't lean out too far!" Moon Man warned. "You may fall off. Now, what do you see?"

"I see into my own house!" Uteritsoq said, amazed. "My wife is sitting on her bench. She is plaiting sinews for thread."

"Her time of mourning must be over," Moon Man said.

"There is a woman sitting with her," said Uteritsoq. "Oh, oh—it is the woman who slammed me against a rock and stole my stomach guts! It's her, the moon spirit!"

"She makes enemies fast; she makes friends fast," Moon Man said.

"Now they are making dolls," Uteritsoq said. "What kind of dolls are they?"

"Duckbill dolls," Moon Man said.

"What can such dolls do?" Uteritsoq asked. "Of what use are they?"

"They can become real children," said Moon Man. "If you put the stone to your ear, you can hear your wife and the moon spirit talk."

Uteritsoq put the stone to his ear. He listened.

"Your husband is stubborn," the moon spirit said.

"Yes, yes, he is," Uteritsoq's wife said. "He can be a terrible fool. I often dream of living in a separate village from him."

"Hey, hey—I don't like the way they speak of me!" Uteritsoq complained.

Uteritsoq looked through the stone again. He looked into his house. Duckbill dolls were fairly spinning from the moon spirit's fingers.

"There are a lot of dolls!" Uteritsoq said in alarm.

"Yes, the old woman works fast," said Moon Man.

"I'm going home to kick that old woman out of my house," said Uteritsoq.

"Well, all right," said Moon Man. "But take some advice. On your way, better stop to catch some fish, some hare, some ptarmigan, some seals, and a few walrus as well. You will have many mouths to feed."

"But there is only my wife and myself to feed!" Uteritsoq said.

"Do as you see fit, then," said Moon Man. "But, remember, the last time you didn't take my advice, you lost your stomach guts."

Uteritsoq peered through the stone again and saw where hare, ptarmigan, seal, and walrus were. Also, he saw where the biggest fish were, just offshore near his village.

"Now, dive through the hole in that stone!" Moon Man said.

Uteritsoq set the stone on the ground, then dove through the hole in it. He landed near some walrus. He hunted them; he cut them up and dragged them along.

He hunted seals, ptarmigan, hare, and caught many fish. He took five days to do this. He lugged and dragged all of it home.

When he stepped into his house, he looked everywhere for the moon spirit, but she was not to be found. The duckbill dolls were all over the place, though.

His wife looked outside. "You have caught enough food for tonight's meal, all right," she said. "But for the days following that, well, you'll need to go hunting again."

"What do you mean?" Uteritsoq said. "There's plenty of food."

"Look, I've prepared a meal for you," his wife said. "You have been on an arduous journey. Eat some food. Then go to sleep. You will need all of your strength tomorrow."

"No, tomorrow I'm going to laze about," Uteritsoq said. "But just now, I am tired."

Uteritsoq ate his meal and fell asleep.

In the morning when he woke, Uteritsoq saw that each and every one of the duckbill dolls had turned into a son or a daughter!

"Father, bring home a walrus! Father, Father, bring us a hare to eat! Father, bring us some fish!" the children cried out. Words of hunger flew out of each of their mouths, and when Uteritsoq looked outside, he discovered that all of the food he had brought home was gone!

"Let your father eat his breakfast," Uteritsoq's wife said. "Then he'll go out hunting."

After eating his breakfast, it took Uteritsoq much of the morning to learn the

names of his new children. Then he set out to his most reliable hunting grounds. When he returned, he had a sled full of walrus, seal, and fish. The children gobbled them all up for supper that night.

After supper the children went to sleep. Uteritsoq said to his wife, "Life has suddenly changed."

"It is good you noticed that," said his wife.

Uteritsoq and his wife fell asleep.

The next morning Uteritsoq took all of his children out into the village to show them off. He gathered the villagers together.

"Son," he said to one of the boys, "fetch me my best fish-jigging pole."

"No!" the boy said stubbornly.

"Daughter," Uteritsoq said to one of the girls, "fetch me my best mukluks."

"No! No! No!" the girl said.

One by one Uteritsoq asked each of his children to fetch something, and each said, "No!"

Delighted to see that the children had much of Uteritsoq's stubbornness, the villagers fell laughing to the ground.

All of the children scattered every which way. It took a long time for the villagers to learn each of their names. As for Uteritsoq, he stomped back home, fetched his best fish-jigging pole, and spent the rest of his day fishing from his kayak. Out in the kayak he had moods. Sometimes he laughed; sometimes he cried. And through it all, he caught a lot of fish. He had very, very good luck.

THE WOLVERINE'S SECRET

IN THE EARLIEST INUIT TIMES, just as now, there was sunlight and moonlight. But the great, sweeping ripples of color shimmering in the night sky, known as the northern lights, did not yet exist.

Now it happened that one thickly overcast night, a wolverine was marauding about. It stalked close to the edge of a village on the tundra near the mouth of the Yukon River. It walked through the village and saw that all the people were asleep. Then, using its magic strength, it leapt up to the moon, pulled the moon down from the sky, shrunk it, and stuffed it into a sack made of caribou hide. Next the wolverine flew back into the sky, pulled down the sun, shrunk it as well, and stuffed it into another sack. The wolverine ran off, far upriver.

At the outskirts of the village, a boy lived alone. He was an orphan. He got along with people all right. He would attend feasts and drum-dances. Mostly, though, he preferred to be with ravens. Much of the day he could be found sitting on an ornate bench he had carved at the entranceway of his hut. He would toss bits of fish to the ravens. Ravens perched on his roof, squalled around his hut, and even walked

59

inside, for ravens are very good at walking as well as flying. This strange boy was talented at raven-talk; he knew the different caws, chortles, coughs, and rasps. He talked things over with the ravens.

Now, in the village there was one man who did not like the orphan. This man was a powerful shaman. He wanted the ravens' magic, but the ravens refused him this magic. He was viciously jealous of the orphan. He wanted to speak with ravens but could not. Trying to befriend the ravens, the shaman would dress up in a robe of raven feathers, squat, and wobble like a raven through the village, all the while saying, "Caw, caw, caw," or "Hic, hic, hic," or "Chah, chhh, chhh," or "Tttt rawhhh!" But the shaman could only *imitate* the ravens, not really talk with them.

"Come on," the shaman would say. "Give me some of your magic!"

But the ravens would only flock off to the orphan's hut. Late into the night, the orphan and ravens would gossip about the shaman. The shaman would listen at the orphan's door. Caws, chortles, rasps, hiccoughs, hisses—yes, the shaman knew full well they were having a fine time of it, mocking and insulting him! He listened in, stone-faced, his heart pounding with rage.

Now, after the wolverine stole the sun and moon, it was almost completely dark in the village. There was a faint glimmer of stars and the snow gave off a little light, too, but in the morning, when the villagers woke, they felt panic and fear and ran about crying, "Things are not familiar! Things are not familiar!"

"There is no sunlight to hunt and fish by!" one man said.

"We will starve!" another said.

"Let's wait and see if the moon comes out!" a woman said.

They huddled together and waited a long, long time. No moon.

"In such darkness," a woman said, "our children may wander off, and we won't be able to find them!"

The shaman stepped up and said, "Build up a big fire! I'll work my magic and bring back the sun and moon!"

Quickly the villagers made a fire. Near the edge of the village, the ravens made a small fire for the orphan to stand near. The orphan and ravens watched from there.

The shaman chanted and danced, he circled with his drum, he muttered secret words—he worked his magic for a long time. But the sun and moon were still not to be seen.

Finally the orphan walked up to the shaman. "What kind of magician are you, anyway?" the boy asked. "You can't even bring back the sun and moon! Why, even I can do that!"

Hearing this, the shaman got so mad that he threw a bucketful of ashes at the boy. The ravens quickly doused the boy with snow—*hssssss!*—but the ashes stuck to the boy and turned to feathers.

"What kind of magician are you, anyway?" the boy asked. "You can't even properly turn me into a raven! I'll show you how!"

The ravens lifted the orphan into the sky, wheeled him about, then put him on the ground again. Now the boy was covered with raven feathers.

"Look!" one woman shouted. "Look at the orphan's feet!"

And everybody saw that the boy now had raven feet!

"It's Raven—the trickster!" the shaman said. "The boss of all the ravens! The troublemaker! It is this trickster who stole the sun and moon!"

Well, the villagers were so wrought up with fear and confusion, they believed the shaman first thing and drove the raven-boy from the village with their fists.

The raven-boy began to fly off to his hut. But as he went he called out, "The shaman is wrong! It was a wolverine who stole the sun and moon. My ravens saw it happen! I'll prove it to you!"

At his hut the raven-boy talked things over with the ravens.

"What can I do to fetch back the sun and moon?" he asked.

"You must set out on a journey," the eldest raven said. "Far, far upriver. For that is where the thief-wolverine lives. Stop along the way at your aunt's house, the aunt you visited just two days ago. But first turn back into a boy, so that she will recognize you."

"I'll take your advice," the boy said, and turned back into a human boy. There was a pile of raven feathers at his feet, which now were human feet again.

The boy set out on his journey. The ravens waited on his bench, on his roof, and inside his house. Carrying an oil lamp, he followed the river. After a while he came to his aunt's house. When he stepped inside, he saw that his aunt wore a new rabbit-fur coat.

"Nephew," she said, "what is the reason for your visit?"

"Did you notice that the sun and moon were gone?" he asked.

"Yes," she said.

"Well, I was falsely accused of stealing the sun and moon," he said. "I was pummeled from my village! Do you have any idea who really took the sun and moon?"

"No, no," the aunt said. "I'm just a poor old woman who lives alone. You are the only one who ever visits me!"

"You are lying!" the boy shouted. "You must know something. Look, here, at your fine, new rabbit-fur coat—you didn't have it the last time I visited, only two

days ago! Only a wolverine could catch enough rabbits in so short a time to make a coat. And you needed more than faint starlight or a cooking fire to sew it by!"

Knowing she was caught in her lie, the orphan's aunt owned up to it. "Yes, nephew, you are right," she said. "I lied to you. A wolverine did smuggle the sun and moon into my house."

"And what bargain did the wolverine make with you?" the boy asked.

"Well, you know how far I wandered upriver in my youth," the aunt said. "As a young girl I often ran away from home and lived for days on my own, far, far upriver. I got a reputation for it. So I learned many secret places, far upriver. When the wolverine offered me the rabbit furs, I told him of a secret place to hide. He gave me the rabbit furs. Then he opened two caribou-hide sacks, letting enough sunlight and moonlight out for me to sew the coat by. I sewed fast. Then the wolverine left to go far, far upriver."

"Where is this hiding place?" the boy asked.

"Between two boulders on the north bank, where the river forks," the aunt said. "You will know you are getting close when you are in an open stretch of tundra and the wind whistles and hisses in your ears. The wind there is fierce."

"Good-bye, then, aunt," the boy said.

"Good-bye, nephew," she said.

The boy quickly set out, far, far upriver. He traveled a long time. He did not sleep at all. He kept moving upriver. The ravens had given him a bundle of food, which he ate along the way.

Finally he came to a place where the wind whistled and hissed in his ears. It was

the fiercest wind he had ever known. The pain and loudness was almost too much to bear. But the boy kept going and soon got to a quiet place. He looked around. There he saw a faint glare of light coming from between two boulders. He walked to the boulders. Between the boulders, just as his aunt had said, was the secret hut of the wolverine. He peered in through a crack. He saw the wolverine in there. He saw the caribou-hide sacks, with the shrunken sun and moon inside them.

Suddenly the wolverine stepped out and began to sweep snow from its hut with a broom made of whale rib and rabbit fur.

The boy walked right up and said, "Are you hoarding the sun and moon?"

"I don't know what you're talking about," the wolverine said. "Go away—you aren't welcome here!"

"Listen, listen, listen," the boy said. "It was so dark in my village, I knew that somebody with great magic had stolen the sun and moon. I traveled all this way to learn from you how to steal so well. You must truly be the best thief on the tundra!"

Hearing such flattery, the wolverine stopped sweeping. The wolverine looked the boy over. "No, no—go away!" the wolverine said. "I've got a lot of sweeping to do. I've got work to do. Go away!"

"I heard a rumor that you could chew down a broom and not choke on the splinters," the boy said.

"And did you believe this rumor?" the wolverine asked.

"No," the boy said.

The wolverine rose to the challenge and immediately chewed down the broom, fur to bone handle, and did not choke on the splinters.

"Indeed, you have a powerful jaw," the boy said. "But now that you no longer have a broom, how could you possibly sweep any sunlight or moonlight out to me?"

"Watch—I'll show you!" the wolverine said.

With this, the wolverine went back inside its hut and soon came sweeping sunlight and moonlight, mixed with snow, out of the hut with its tail!

Quickly the boy seized the snow, packed it into snowballs, and hurled them into the sky!

Wonderful—and frightening—shimmering colors appeared! Horizon to zenith, the sky was awash with silver light tinged with red, all rippling down and across. What's more, you could hear the sky crackle with light!

Having worked such magic, the boy turned back to the hut, but the wolverine was not to be seen. When the boy peered inside, he found the wolverine cowering in a corner, whimpering.

"What's this?" the boy asked. "A wolverine is fearless! A wolverine can snarl wolves away from a caribou they have hunted down! A wolverine can crack bones apart! A wolverine is a powerful animal!"

"All of that is true," the wolverine said. "Don't tell anyone my secret—I am only afraid of getting hit by snowballs!"

"How can that be?" the boy asked.

"Just look at me—shivering in my hut!" the wolverine said. "You threw a snowball; I shivered in my hut. That's how it is."

Hearing this, the boy worked fast to make a pile of snowballs. He spit on the snowballs one by one, which caused them to freeze faster and harder. Then he pelted the wolverine, who cringed and whimpered.

The boy ran into the hut, dragged out the sacks containing the sun and moon, and set them outside on the snow. He mixed sunlight and moonlight in with more snow. Then he hurled a snowball at the wolverine. He kept the door of the hut open.

Then he threw a snowball into the sky, threw one at the wolverine, threw another

into the sky, on and on. Each time a snowball was flung into the sky, it shimmered the northern lights brightly. Each time a snowball hit the wolverine, the wolverine's whimpering grew louder.

The boy let loose loud raven squawks and caws, echoing them out, calling in the ravens from his hut. Soon the ravens arrived.

"Help me carry these caribou-hide sacks back to the village," the boy said. Then he turned into a raven and flew with the other ravens back to the village, dangling the sun and moon.

The villagers gathered around.

"First, I'll put the moon back in the sky," the raven-boy told the villagers. He flew the caribou-hide sack holding the moon up into the sky. There, he took a deep breath and blew into the moon, which made it return to its old size. Then he flew back to the ground. Next he flew the caribou-hide sack containing the sun up to the opposite part of the sky, blew into the sun, and the sun returned to its normal size. The raven-boy set it down below the horizon, then flew back to his village. And then he turned into a human boy again.

"You see!" the shaman cried out. "This boy stole the sun and moon! He put us in darkness, so that from now on we'll be afraid of him! Let's kick him out of the village again!"

"No—wait!" the boy said. "I'll work my magic and make it so that all of the villagers here can understand the talk of ravens, just this once. Now—it is done. Ask the ravens who stole the sun and moon!"

"Who stole the sun and moon?" one woman asked the ravens.

"Wolverine!" the ravens said together. "Wolverine!"

"Wolverine, wolverine, wolverine, wolverine, wolverine, wolverine, wolverine, wolverine, wolverine—," the villagers heard, as each one asked the ravens who had stolen the sun and moon.

"From now on," the eldest man in the village said, "this boy will take care of magic goings-on around here!"

"What about me?" the shaman cried.

Hearing this, the ravens flocked at the shaman, clipping his ears with their beaks, chasing him from the village.

That night there was a great feast. The village was celebrating the return of the sun and moon. The boy told of the birth of the northern lights. He told everything that had happened on his journey, far, far upriver. Yet he did not give away the wolverine's secret. "Now and then," he said, "now and then, these shimmering lights will appear in the sky!"

After this, village life was much the same. The boy returned to his hut, and all through his long life preferred the companionship of ravens. Yes, he attended feasts and drum-dances, and when needed he worked powerful and good magic, but most of the time he could be found sitting on his bench. Sometimes he was human; sometimes he was raven. Sometimes he traveled far, far upriver. There were many times a wolverine came around to try to steal the sun and moon again—it seems that wolverines never stop trying to ransack the sky. Each time this happened, though, he quickly packed snowballs and chased the wolverine across the tundra.

THE GIRL WHO WATCHED
IN THE NIGHTTIME

I N THE SIBERIAN coastal village of Unisak, there lived a beautiful girl who each night stayed awake until dawn. She would whittle ivory and bone toys, sing to herself, and otherwise keep occupied. She lived with her parents. Their house was on the seaside of the village. In the very middle of the night, she would set out under the stars to look in on each of her ten cousins—five girls, five boys. To see each one safely asleep gave peace to her heart. She watched her cousins in the nighttime. Then she would walk home. In the morning her parents would find her curled up asleep. Bone and ivory toys would be scattered about.

One night, just as she got back to her house, she heard an argument going on inside. She listened at the door.

"I want to take your daughter to my house and keep her there until she is old enough to marry," a man said.

The girl recognized the voice. It belonged to Steam-Man. Steam-Man was ugly and bent-over and had feet as hard as reindeer hooves. He spent much of his time concocting dyes out of ocher, bark, berries, and reindeer dung. He would wallow his shirts and trousers in cauldrons of dyes, and when the clothes were ready, he would wear them around the village. Because the reindeer dung had soaked into the clothes, Steam-Man always stank!

Do you want to know how Steam-Man got his name? Well, each night he would fill a cauldron with water, boil the water over a fire, and suspend himself by magic in the steam. He would hover there, in the steam. It looked frightening. If he missed a night of hovering in steam, he would be stiff and complain loudly of bone aches. His eyes would roll wildly, his skin would get parched and his hoof-feet cracked.

Listening through the door, the girl was horrified at the thought of marrying Steam-Man and was happy to hear her father reply, "Stay away from my daughter!"

"You refuse my request?" Steam-Man asked.

"Go away, Steam-Man," the father said. "You're hideous. Leave my house at once! You are stinking it up!"

"I can work magic," Steam-Man said. "I can work magic against this village!"

"What magic can you work?" asked the father. "The only magic you have is to sit in the air above your steam cauldron."

"We'll see about that," said Steam-Man. He walked out the door.

Steam-Man stalked off into the night. The girl, who was crouched hiding to one side of the door, smelled him as he went past. She waited until she heard her father snoring, then went inside. She carved ivory toys until morning, all the while singing:

All is well,
sleeping cousins.
My sleeping cousins,
do not worry,
for all is well.

The very next day when Steam-Man was out gathering reindeer droppings in buckets, the girl's father snuck into Steam-Man's house and stole his cauldron. He hid the cauldron among his own reindeer in their corral.

When Steam-Man returned to his house, he cried out, "My steam cauldron is gone!" He was furious. He stomped from house to house. At each door he shouted, "Do you have my cauldron? If I don't take a steam bath, my bones ache. If my bones ache, I'm in a poisonous mood!"

"Maybe it's in somebody's reindeer corral?" the people in each house replied.

"Am I to believe that reindeer stole my cauldron?" Steam-Man would say.

Steam-Man asked after his cauldron at every house, except that of the girl who watched her cousins in the nighttime. He stood at the edge of the village. He held his fists in the air. He cursed the village, then set out into the forest.

That night as usual, the girl set down her ivory and bone toys and went to look in on her cousins. Nearest to her house was that of her boy-cousin who slept using his folded hands as a pillow. She watched him sleep a short while.

The next house over, she sat by her girl-cousin, the one who embroidered belts better than anyone. Next house over slept her girl-cousin who embroidered belts almost as well.

Next house over, the girl looked in on her boy-cousin with close-cropped hair. Next house over slept the boy-cousin who once put a bucket over a reindeer's head. Next house over, she touched the forehead of her girl-cousin who was often given to fevers. Next house over, she tugged lightly at the hair of another of her boy-cousins, the best wrestler in the village; she knew that if she tugged his hair when he was awake, he would wrestle her to the ground. She watched him sleep a short while.

Next house over slept Bruise-Boy, her cousin whose shins were always bruised from getting kicked by reindeer. She rubbed salve into his shins. She then went to the next house over, where her girl-cousin who fashioned whale-vertebrae lamps slept surrounded by whale-vertebrae lamps, each with its container of oil.

Lastly the girl visited her girl-cousin who chattered her teeth like spoons. She did not chatter every night—just some nights. Tonight this girl-cousin chattered her teeth only a little.

Now the girl had visited all her cousins. She had seen them sleep in familiar ways. She set out for home. Along the way she stopped at her father's reindeer corral. She stood at the fence. She looked and saw steam cloud out of the reindeers' nostrils in the cold night air. She listened and heard the reindeer click their hooves against Steam-Man's cauldron. Dawn light was on the sea horizon. She went home to sleep.

Village life went on and on, and Steam-Man was nowhere to be seen. Each night the girl whittled toys. Each night she watched her cousins sleep. Each night, on her way home, she stopped to see the reindeers' nostril-steam, to hear them click their hooves against Steam-Man's cauldron. Each night she sang:

> *All is well,*
> *sleeping cousins.*
> *My sleeping cousins,*
> *do not worry,*
> *for all is well.*

Winter arrived. There was snow on the ground. The girl bundled up warmly

before visiting her cousins in their houses and the reindeer in her father's corral. Her heart was peaceful.

But one night, deep into winter, she saw a startling thing. There, leading up to the house of one of her boy-cousins, the one with close-cropped hair, were fox tracks! She stepped inside the house. She threw aside the blankets and discovered that her boy-cousin was missing!

She ran about the village, searching, searching, but could not find the cousin with close-cropped hair. She even looked inside Steam-Man's cauldron, which the reindeer had nicked with their hooves and turned upside down. She searched all night.

Near morning she ran back and woke up Close-Cropped Hair's mother and father, her aunt and uncle. "Your son is gone!" she cried.

They all hurried outside. They looked at the fox tracks. Both her aunt and uncle threw themselves to the ground, sobbing.

"Did you see anything suspicious last night?" her uncle finally asked.

"Only these fox tracks," she said.

A search party was sent out, across the taiga, into the forest, but it had no luck in finding the boy.

Now, it happened that each night a different cousin was kidnapped. The girl would rush from house to house, hoping to discover the kidnapper in the act, but she was always too late. The village relied on her keeping watch in the nighttime, and she blamed herself for the kidnappings and was very sad.

The boy who slept on his folded hands was missing. The girl who embroidered

belts better than anyone was missing. The girl who embroidered belts almost as well was missing. The boy who had put a bucket over a reindeer's head was missing. Oh, it was terrible, terrible. The girl given to fevers was missing. The boy with shin bruises was missing. The girl who fashioned whale-vertebrae lamps was missing. The girl who chattered her teeth was missing.

"Which of your cousins is left?" the girl's father asked.

"Only the boy who is the best wrestler in the village," she said.

That night it snowed heavily. The girl walked around and around the house of the wrestling cousin. She watched for anything suspicious. All night she heard her cousin's moans, so loud they shook the house. Her wrestling cousin was sick from fear of being the next one kidnapped. He would neither eat nor drink. He was dying.

The girl made some broth. She fed it to her cousin. This gave him a bit of strength, but life was fading from him. His mother and father tried different medicines, but none worked. The wrestling cousin stopped talking altogether. He only mumbled and drooled. He was a pathetic sight.

As the snow fell, the girl built a snow hut and crouched inside. She stuck her thumbs through its wall so that she could see out. The snow fell and fell. The night was very still. All the girl could hear was the wrestling boy's moans and her father's reindeer kicking Steam-Man's cauldron. But then the girl heard, "Qua, qua, qua!"

It was the voice of a fox.

Now the girl, who had plaited a rope, stepped outside the snow hut. When the fox approached her cousin's door, she flung the rope and perfectly snagged the fox by its legs. She pulled the rope fast, tripping the fox.

"Why did you come here?" the girl asked the fox.

"To kidnap the wrestling boy, of course," the fox said.

"Who do you work for?" asked the girl.

"Steam-Man," replied the fox.

Hearing this, the girl tied the fox to the house. She went inside, put on her wrestling cousin's clothes, covered her cousin with two extra blankets, and, dragging the fox behind her, set out for the forest.

"You'll get lost out here," said the fox.

"If you don't lead me to Steam-Man," the girl said, "I'll choke you with this rope."

The fox ran a short distance ahead—just to the end of the rope. The fox sniffed along the snow and finally drew the girl close to Steam-Man's hut, deep among the trees.

"Now, call out to Steam-Man," the girl said. "Say that you have kidnapped the wrestling boy."

"Qua, qua, qua!" the fox barked. "Steam-Man, it is me, the fox. I have kidnapped the wrestling boy! Come see!"

Steam-Man came laughing out of his hut. When Steam-Man got close, the girl leapt on him. He tried to kick her with his hoof-feet, but she was too quick for him. She tied him to the fox. Then she looked inside the hut. Her cousins were not there. She dragged Steam-Man and the fox back to the village.

A tribunal was held. Everyone in the village was there. Steam-Man and the fox were placed in the middle of the circle of villagers.

The girl stepped forth. "What have you both done?" she asked.

"Kidnapped nine children," Steam-Man owned up.

"And where are they now—the children?" the girl asked.

"Qua!—out in the forest!" cried the fox. "Qua, qua, qua!"

"If you let us go free, I'll show you exactly where in the forest the children are hidden," Steam-Man pleaded.

"Fox," said the girl, "if you do not lead us to the children, I will place you in Steam-Man's cauldron and have my father's reindeer kick it around until you are driven mad!"

"I'm not afraid of that!" the fox snapped.

"We'll see," said the girl.

She tethered the fox's four feet together and stuffed the fox into Steam-Man's cauldron. She rolled the cauldron back out amid her father's reindeer. The reindeer kicked the cauldron all around the corral. "Qua, qua, qua!" the villagers all shouted.

In a short time the fox called out, "The children are at the far end of the forest, in a snow hut next to the birch trees that have the biggest knotholes!"

Quickly, a search party was sent for the children. It found them and brought them back. All of the girl's aunts and uncles jumped about with happiness at the sight of their children. The children were bundled up and fed broth. They sipped a little at first, then lifted the bowls to their mouths. Steam-Man had fed them only bits of bark, and they were starving. After gulping down many bowls of broth, each cousin ate some reindeer meat, fish, and biscuits.

"This feast had by my kidnapped cousins, safe with their families again, brings me great joy!" the girl said.

Everyone circled Steam-Man.

"Why did you do such an odious thing?" a villager asked.

"To ransom the children for the young girl's hand in marriage," Steam-Man said.

"First, we'll roll you in reindeer dung," said the girl.

Her aunts and uncles rolled Steam-Man in reindeer dung.

Then the girl rolled Steam-Man to the corral. She stuffed him into his steam cauldron. She opened the gate. She snapped a whip across the rumps of the reindeer. The reindeer kicked the cauldron through the gate, out on the taiga toward the forest. The girl untied the fox, which ran after the echoing cauldron.

"Qua, qua, qua!" the villagers called after the fox.

Many years went by. Steam-Man stayed away from the village. Still, the girl watched over her cousins in the nighttime. She knew that Steam-Man might hold a grudge and plot to kidnap her cousins again.

One night, a night of many stars in the sky, the girl, who had become a beautiful woman, was on her way to a cousin's house. It was the cousin who was still given to fevers, though she, too, was a young woman now. Along the path to her cousin's house, the young woman who watched in the nighttime saw fox tracks! The sight of the tracks quickened her heart. She hurried on.

Up ahead she saw a startling sight. At her cousin's doorstep a man was knotting up the legs of a fox!

"Qua, qua, qua!" the fox cried, but the man stuffed snow into the fox's mouth. He slung the fox over his shoulder.

"Who are you?" the young woman asked. She saw that he was a handsome young man.

"I'm from a neighboring village, just up the coast," he said. "I'm good at making knots. I make knots that can keep a tent upright on its stakes in the fiercest wind,

knots that hold a skin-boat to the rocks. And see—I've knotted up the legs of this fox. It was marauding around my village, stealing food. I followed it here. I caught it and was about to carry it off."

"Yes, I believe I've heard of you," the young woman said. "Aren't you most especially known for knotting dog harnesses?"

"Yes," he said.

"Well, I have a lot of cousins to visit," the young woman said. "Please let me pass. I've got to put my hand on my cousin's forehead."

"Why is that?" the handsome young man asked.

"She is given to fevers," the young woman said. "I'm going to see if she has one tonight."

"Let me go with you," the young man said.

"Well, all right," the young woman said. "But put that fox down on the snow. Don't bring a fox near my cousin, its legs knotted up or not. I don't trust foxes."

"Are you afraid that your cousin will catch lice?" the man asked.

"No," the young woman said.

"Well, are you afraid that the fox will bite your cousin?" he asked.

"No," the young woman said.

"What are you afraid of, then?" he asked.

"That the fox will kidnap my cousin," the young woman said.

"No, not this fox!" the man said. "You're thinking of the fox that works for Steam-Man. No, no, don't worry. This fox only steals scraps of food. Now, there's a

fox down the coast who chews through dog harnesses. There's a fox even farther down the coast who drags off drying salmon. And some foxes prefer to shun human villages altogether; they don't cause a bit of trouble."

The handsome young man tightened the fox's leg-knots, then packed snow around the fox.

"There," he said, "this fox can't get away."

"All right, then," the young woman said. "Let's go inside. Be very quiet."

Inside the house she knelt next to her sleeping cousin. She put her hand on her cousin's forehead. "I think she has a fever tonight," the young woman said.

"Let me touch her forehead," the man said.

He reached over and touched the sleeping cousin's forehead.

"Yes, she has a fever," he said. "I can cure it."

"How?" the young woman whispered.

"Watch," he said.

He opened up a sack made of reindeer hide. He reached inside and took out some berries, roots, and a small figure whittled from ivory. He held the figure close to the young woman's face; she saw that it was a tiny white fox!

"What is that?" the young woman asked.

"A magic figure," the man said. "It was given to me by a fox. You see, there are some foxes who work powerfully good magic. One such fox gave me this ivory figure."

"Try to cure my cousin's fever, then," said the young woman.

The handsome young man mixed the berries and roots together in a bowl. He   *83*

added some water. Lifting the fevered cousin's head, he dripped a little medicinal broth into her mouth. The cousin woke and sipped some more.

"Who is this man?" the cousin asked.

"He's from a village up the coast," the young woman who watched in the nighttime said. "He's a knot maker. Also, he can tell a good fox from a bad one."

"And he has cured my fever," the cousin said.

"Not quite," the young man said.

Saying that, he waved the ivory fox over the cousin's face.

"There, now you are cured," he said. And from that night forward, this cousin never had a fever again.

In the morning the young woman who watched in the nighttime took the handsome young man to meet her mother and father.

"Mother, Father," she said, "this man has a gift for you."

"Very well, then," the father said. "Let's have a look."

The handsome young man set the knotted-up fox on the floor.

"You have knotted up this fox very well," said the father.

"Thank you," said the young man.

"Father, Mother," the young woman said to her parents. "He is from a village up the coast. He is an expert in knots. What's more, he can tell a good fox from a bad one. And he can cure fevers."

"Is all of this true?" the mother asked.

"Yes," said the handsome young man.

"Very well, then," the father said. "Go and fetch *your* mother, father, aunts, uncles—all of your family. We'll provide a feast."

The young man was gone for ten days. When he returned he had his mother, father, sisters, brothers, aunts, uncles, grandparents, and cousins with him.

They held a big feast. They ate salmon, berries, reindeer meat, biscuits, and stews of many sorts.

It was a night full of stars in the sky. Everyone stayed up late, laughing and talking, eating and drinking. Then, in the middle of the night, the young woman who watched in the nighttime and the handsome young man were married.

They lived together in a house on the seaside of the village. Every night she whittled ivory toys, then went house to house, looking in on her cousins. She watched them sleep. Should a kidnap fox, a salmon-thief fox, or a harness-chewing fox come around, she would hurry back, wake her husband, and he would knot the fox's legs.

In all the villages up and down the coast, she was known as the woman who watched in the nighttime; he was known as the man who knotted up foxes in the nighttime.

They had three children and lived to be very, very old.

THE MAN WHO
MARRIED A SEAGULL

F AR NORTH, between two inlets, lived a seagull and her two uncles. She liked to circle over the nearby Inuit village. She liked to watch what the human beings did all day.

One morning she said, "Uncles, I want to become a human being."

"Why?" asked one uncle.

"Because I'm curious," she said.

"And what else?" asked the other uncle.

"Because you treat me badly," she said. "You steal my food, and you peck at me so often my feathers are torn and shabby, which makes it difficult to fly. And the way you whistle through your nostrils annoys me."

"Very well," said one uncle. "But someday we'll come to fetch you back."

The uncles worked some magic and turned their niece into a beautiful young woman. The uncles flew off. They keened high in the air. Then they were gone. The young woman stood on a drift of ice.

Now, it happened that a very fine and handsome young hunter was out in his kayak looking for seals nearby. He squinted his eyes, staring up ahead. He was surprised to see what at first he thought was a seal standing on its flippers. As he paddled closer, he saw it was a beautiful young woman dressed in a coat of gull feathers. He maneuvered his kayak around drifts of ice, and when he drew up to her, he said, "How did you get out here? Where is your kayak?"

"What's important is that I'll go back to your village with you," she said.

The man certainly agreed. She climbed into the kayak and he paddled north along the coast to his village. When they reached the village, they got out of the kayak. "Let's go meet my mother and father," the man said.

"Wait!" said the young woman. "Do you want to marry me?"

The young man did not have to think very long. "Yes," he said.

"Then go get me some clothes," she said. "I can't bear this feather coat."

"All right," the man said.

He hurried into his village. He went into his cousin's house and said, "Cousin, the woman I'm going to marry has only a shabby, flea-ridden coat made of gull feathers. She's standing at the edge of our village right now. Can I have one of your coats and a pair of boots? If I don't bring these to her, I'm sure she won't marry me."

His cousin gave him the clothes. He ran back and handed the coat and boots to the young woman. She put them on, then threw her feather coat into the sea. It drifted away.

The wedding took place the next day. The new couple moved into a small house on the riverbank, just inland from the sea. The man was a great hunter. He brought in seals and fish. His wife plaited fishing line expertly, and she often caught fish from the riverbank. They had many visitors and they visited the man's parents often. This is how life went. They were happy. The only sadness was that the husband's two uncles had been whirled to the sea bottom by a waterspout early in the summer, and he missed them terribly.

Winter came, they lived through it well, and then it was close to the ice-breakup. One day the husband went to where the river met the sea, his favorite seal-hunting spot, and his wife went to fish from the riverbank. While she was busy fishing, she looked up and saw two gulls floating high in the air. Greatly alarmed, she ran home.

Her husband came back without a seal but with five large fish. Right away his wife prepared them. The husband sat and talked with her. They were just talking when suddenly they looked up and saw two men standing in their doorway.

The husband leapt for his harpoon, then stood with it at the ready. "I don't recognize you," the husband said to the men.

"We are your wife's uncles," one of the men answered.

"Uncles!" the man said. "My wife never mentioned that she had uncles. How do I know that you're telling me the truth?"

One uncle held out the shabby feather coat. "You see," he said, "we found our niece's coat far out to sea. We wondered as to her whereabouts. We've been searching for her. Finally we came here."

"That's her old coat, all right," the husband said. He turned to his wife. "Are these your uncles?"

"Yes," she said. She had been so happy; she could not bear to tell her husband that she was a gull and that these were gull-uncles, too.

"Very well," the husband said. "Uncles. Uncles. We need uncles around here. My own uncles were drowned by a waterspout."

"That's bad news," one of the visiting uncles said.

"Come in. Sit down," the husband said. "We have plenty of fish. Stay for a meal."

The uncles each sat in an opposite corner. The husband noticed that they had very thin faces. His wife placed the fish in the middle of the house. "Visiting uncles," the husband said, "go ahead—eat!"

One uncle circled the fish, then all but pecked at one, finally pinching off a small bit without using his hands at all! Once he had this tiny piece in his mouth, he quickly retreated to his corner. But no sooner had he done so than the other uncle swooped across and nabbed the fish-bit right from his mouth! The thieving uncle then flailed the air with his arms, scurried back to his own corner, and quickly gobbled down the bit of fish.

"Uncles! Uncles!" the husband said, startled. "There's more than enough food for everyone! No need to fight over it."

Still, this went on throughout the meal. One uncle would warily eye the other, then suddenly snap up a piece of fish. When the wife, husband, and uncles finally had their shares, one uncle said to his niece, "Hey, hey—where are the intestines?"

"I scraped them out," the young wife said. "I threw them to our dogs."

"What about the eyeballs?" asked the other uncle. "And where are the fish tails?"

"All to the dogs," said the woman.

"You've forgotten how to prepare fish properly," the other uncle said. "You'd better come back to our village with us right away."

"I wouldn't even let my wife *visit* a village where they eat fish intestines!" the husband said.

"Why not leave now, uncles," said the wife. "It's clear that I can't prepare fish the way you like. You're not pleased. Why not leave?"

"How long do you expect to stay, anyway?" the husband asked.

"Just a few days," one uncle said.

"Very well, then," said the husband. "Ungrateful uncles are still uncles, and next time we'll leave the fish intestines, eyeballs, and tails for you. But you must eat them outside, where we don't have to watch."

That night the husband and wife slept in their customary place. The uncles started out falling asleep in separate corners. But in the middle of the night, the husband heard a sound like a broom brushing atop the house. He went outside. Looking up, he saw the two uncles, eyes closed, sitting upright on the roof. They each had on feather-tipped mittens and were moving their hands slightly in sleep, which accounted for the noise. The husband went back inside. He lay down and stayed awake all night, listening to the uncles on the roof.

The husband found much of this strange but said nothing of it. The next morning he said, "I'm going to hunt seals." Carrying his kayak, he set out.

As soon as he was out of sight, the uncles walked in and began to talk. They chattered, gossiped, and complained all day; all day, chatter, gossip, complaints. What's more, when their niece went out fishing and returned with ten fish, the uncles immediately stood on the fish, bending down and tearing them apart with their teeth, snapping the skin off, and letting pieces fly and spatter the walls. The uncles ate the entrails, stomachs, eyeballs, and tails, too. The niece scrubbed the walls, all the while harangued by the uncles, who chattered and chattered and would not stop. Finally she lay down and fell asleep. She suffered from uncle-exhaustion. She tossed and turned in uncomfortable sleep. The uncles sat in opposite corners, gabbing and nostril-whistling.

Now, it happened that all this time the husband was out in his favorite seal-hunting inlet. It was the beginning of the great ice-breakup; it was still bitterly cold out, but the sun was shining for longer each day. It had been nearly a year since the man had first seen the beautiful woman out on the ice. Already much of the inlet

was clear of ice, but, still, great jagged floes were about, and the man had to be careful, for if he got too close, a floe could suck him under. He had just broken into a clear stretch of water when he saw an unusual thing: a kayak full of ghosts.

Now, he had heard about such a sight since he was a child. His mother and father had each said, "One day you might see a kayak full of ghosts." A number of other hunters had reported seeing one, too. But none of the others said they had gotten this close. The man was frightened. But he was curious, too. Finally he decided to paddle right up to the ghosts' kayak.

As he drew near, the ghosts looked directly at him. Then, speaking in a single voice, the ghosts said, "Your wife is a gull."

Without another word, the ghosts paddled away. The man admired the way they guided their kayak so effortlessly around the jagged floes.

All the rest of his hunting day, the man pondered what the ghosts had said. The words "Your wife is a gull" kept swirling around in his mind.

Your wife is a gull. Your wife is a gull. Your wife is a gull.

That day the man caught some fish, but he didn't catch a seal.

When he returned home, the young man saw that his wife was asleep.

"Asleep, and it's not yet suppertime," he said. He jostled his wife awake. "Wife, are you ill?"

"No," she said, "I'm uncle-exhausted."

"Let's kick them out, then," the husband said.

Right away the husband pushed the uncles toward the door. They fought him with all their might. The uncles pecked at him and beat at his shoulders with their

arms. The uncles were wearing down the husband, exhausting him. But he managed to get them outside and shut the door behind them. In a short while the wife threw a biscuit out. She and her husband watched as the uncles fought over every crumb.

The husband and wife were uncle-exhausted down to their very bones. Too tired to even eat supper, they lay down and went to sleep. But in the middle of the night, the man woke to a crunching sound. Pretending still to be asleep, he peeked open his eyes and saw his wife picking clean a fish skeleton, using only her teeth. He closed his eyes but could not sleep. Soon his wife lay down next to him again.

Early the next morning, when the man stepped outside, he noticed that it was much colder than the previous day and that snow had fallen. It seemed that winter had come back full force. Some years it happens that suddenly the inlets freeze up even though it is almost summer, and then people have to wait for a second ice-breakup.

The man harnessed up his sled dogs and set out to hunt seals. Far from home, he saw the kayak full of ghosts again, paddling between jagged floes closing up fast. He snapped his whip above the dogs, drove them out on a peninsula of ice, drawing close to the kayak. He now saw that the kayak was trapped between floes. The ghosts had been caught by the sudden freeze-up.

"The visitor-uncles are gulls, too," the ghosts said. "They want to take your wife and turn her back into a gull again. They have such magic. Chisel us out of the ice, and we'll tell you how to get rid of the gull-uncles."

"Very well," said the man.

He chiseled and chiseled, finally breaking the kayak loose. When they were free, the ghosts said, "Don't feed the uncles inside your house. Instead, scatter biscuits and fish tails down by the sea. We will make the air colder and colder and colder yet. What happens next will please you."

"Good-bye, then, ghosts," the man said.

"Good-bye, hunter," the ghosts said.

"Don't feed the uncles inside your house. Don't feed the uncles inside your house. Don't feed the uncles inside your house," the man sang as he traveled back to his house.

When he got home, the man saw that his wife had let the uncles back inside. She was asleep. The gull-uncles had covered her with a feather coat! Angered by this sight, the husband pulled the coat away and threw it outside to his dogs, who tore it to pieces, feathers flying every which way. Despite all the commotion, his wife was so tired she did not even wake up. The man took some biscuits and fish, then left the house. Outside he cut off the fish tails, tossed the fish themselves to the dogs, and just as the ghosts had instructed, scattered the biscuits and fish tails down by the sea. Then he returned home.

"Uncles," he said. "There's no more food in my house. But there are biscuits and fish tails down by the sea!"

The gull-uncles chattered excitedly, then hurried out. Keeping out of sight, the husband followed. At the sea edge the husband hid behind a boulder and watched the uncles quarrel over each biscuit. They skirmished over each fish tail. They were so busy fighting and arguing, they failed to notice how cold it was getting. Ferocious winds careened off the sea ice. Even while buffeted by wind, the uncles kept on fighting over the last biscuit. They were getting worn out. It sometimes happened that the uncles could exhaust each other.

In such plunging cold, the gull-uncles' breaths were puffing out and forming fog-capes over their heads. The breaths were becoming solid now, icing up, settling hard on the uncles' bodies. Breath after struggling breath fogged out of their nostrils and

mouths, hardening fast in the cold air. As they became weighted down by capes of their own frozen breaths, the uncles were less and less able to move. Finally they were frozen all the way through.

The gull-uncles had frozen. To finish things off, the ghosts worked more magic and turned the gull-uncles into rocks. Today you can still see those very rocks at the edge of the sea.

It had gotten so cold that the husband could barely trudge home; he almost froze in his tracks. Still, he managed to get to his house and push open the door. Immediately he saw his wife choking, and when he reached into her throat, he pulled out a complete fish skeleton.

"Thank you, husband," she said.

"Do you ever want to become a gull again?" the husband asked.

"I'm ashamed I didn't tell you before that I was a gull," she said. "Still, no, I want to stay a human being."

"Fine, then," he said.

"You look cold and tired," she said. "Did my uncles wear you out again?"

"Yes," he said.

"Where are they?" she asked.

"Down at the sea edge," he said.

"Will they be having supper with us?" she asked.

"No," he said. "They are rocks now. They won't be having supper again at all."

"I see," she said. "We'll have a good meal together. Tomorrow let's go down to
the sea and watch for the ice-breakup."

"Good idea," the husband said.

The next morning, early, the husband and wife sat near the uncle-size rocks and watched the ice-breakup.

"An ice-breakup, a freeze-up, a second ice-breakup," said the wife. "That is a lot to see in one spring, isn't it?"

"Yes, it is," said the husband.

They sat awhile. In the far distance they saw the kayak full of ghosts drift out to sea. Then they went home.

The wife never turned back into a gull. In time the husband and wife had a daughter, then a son, then another daughter, none of whom were gulls.

HOME AMONG THE GIANTS

ONE DAY A GIANT was taking enormous steps across the tundra, traveling in the roundabout way of giants, when he decided to rest. He sat on some boulders. Right away he heard a whimpering.

"Who's crying?" he asked.

There was no answer.

The giant stood, flicked away the boulders. They rolled all the way to the sea. The giant discovered a small boy huddled where the boulders had been.

"Don't press me flat with your thumb," the boy pleaded.

"I'm not going to press you flat," said the giant.

"I'm lost," the boy said.

"That makes sense, since I haven't seen a human being in this territory for years," the giant said. "Once in a while a ten-legged polar bear happens by, and messenger ravens bring in news from other places, but mostly I see other giants out here."

"My parents and I were separated many days ago," said the boy.

"How did that happen?" asked the giant.

"We were paddling our kayak down the river, when another giant reached out and plucked us up," the boy said. "He placed my mother and father on one side of the river and me on the other. Then he hastened in a thick fog that surrounded us, and I couldn't see my mother and father. I shouted, but the fog swallowed my voice. I started to walk. When the fog lifted, I saw that I'd wandered far from the river. I saw the boulders. I huddled between them. When I saw you walking toward me, I thought you were that same giant coming after me, and that you'd press me flat with your thumb."

"Tell me," the giant said, "was this particular giant straddling the river when you first saw him?"

"Yes," said the boy.

"I *know* that giant," the giant said. "He likes to straddle rivers, he likes to eat ten or so whales at a time, and you are right, he also likes to press things flat with his thumb."

"Well, from a great distance, all of you giants look alike," the boy said. "But close-up I see that you are each different."

"You look weak," said the giant. "How long since you've eaten?"

"Four days," the boy said.

"Well, let's go to the river," said the giant. "There I'll scoop up a beluga whale when it comes in to feed and we'll eat. Then we'll search for your mother and father."

The giant set the boy on his shoulder. He took a few steps, and they arrived at the river—today it is called the Churchill River. There they saw the giant who liked to

straddle rivers. He already had five whales stacked up. And he was pressing boulders flat with his thumb.

"My travel companion here is very hungry," the first giant called out to the river-straddling giant. "I see that you have captured five beluga whales. Why not step aside and let me scoop a sixth one out of the river?"

"No!" the river-straddling giant bellowed.

"Well, then, let us take a few bites out of one of your whales," the first giant said.

"No!" the river-straddling giant shouted.

The first giant set the boy down in a safe place, then leapt on the river-straddling giant. They began to wrestle. There were great rumbling and slamming noises. There was thunderous stomping. They threw each other to the ground, tore at each other's hair, bit each other on the shins. The fighting went on throughout much of the morning. Finally the river-straddling giant was pinned to the ground.

"This giant has thick boots on," the first giant called out to the boy. "That's because he's got soft feet and can't walk across rough ground without boots. Here, boy, take my knife and cut his bootstraps. We'll take his boots, so he can't follow us."

The boy took up the giant's knife and tried to cut the bootstraps, but they were too thick. The boy could only nick and scratch them. He kept at it but failed to cut through.

"I'm getting tired, holding this giant down," the first giant said. "Hurry up!"

"I'm tired, too," said the boy. "I'm having no luck."

"Let me go!" the river-straddling giant cried out. "Let me go!"

Then a very surprising thing happened. The wife of the river-straddling giant   *103* appeared on the horizon; with just a few steps she reached the river. Seeing her husband pinned to the ground, she said, "What's this? What's going on here?"

"Help me, wife!" the river-straddling giant said.

But instead of helping him, the giant's wife tugged off her husband's boots, slid out the straps, and tied up the two fighting giants at the wrists and ankles.

"Don't press me flat with your thumb," the boy begged.

"I won't," she said.

She turned to the tied-up giants. "You both should be ashamed! Look at this boy. He's starving. And all you can do is wrestle! I'll catch something for him to eat."

Having said that, she reached into the river and clutched a beluga whale, knocked it on the head with her fist, and set it on the ground. Then she nabbed a seal and some small fish, knocked them on the heads, and set them next to the whale.

"Let's eat," she said to the boy.

The river-straddling giant's wife and the boy ate and ate until all of the freshly caught food was gone.

"I was very hungry," the boy said.

"I was very hungry as well," the river-straddling giant's wife said.

The two of them broke into loud laughter, but the tied-up giants didn't think any of this was funny at all.

Now she cut up some of her husband's whales, set the meat on the ground, and leaned over to untie the first giant. She did not untie her husband.

"Here's some food for your journey," she said to the boy and the first giant. "Now, begone with you!"

"What about your angry husband?" the boy asked.

"I'll see to it that he doesn't follow you," she said, and with a sharp kick she rolled her husband all the way to the sea.

The boy and the giant traveled all day. When dusky light settled over the land,

they made camp. The giant took a big seal-oil lamp from his belt and lit it. They sat

close to the lamp, nibbling on different-size pieces of whale. After supper they grew sleepy. But before they dozed off, a raven landed next to the boy.

"Cawwggghhh!" the raven said. "Boy, your mother and father are searching across the tundra for you. Cawwggghhh! Cawwggghhh!"

"Where are they?" the boy asked.

But the raven flew off.

The boy wept, for he missed his parents deeply.

"Let me help you think of something else," the giant said. "You'll recall my telling you about a ten-legged polar bear. Well, it's a rarely seen bear. I don't know why it has ten feet, but it does. It has so many feet that when it runs, its feet sometimes get tangled up and it falls down. This is why it spends so much time in the water. When it walks, it's fine. But if it tries to run, its legs get all tangled. Now, let me warn you. Early tomorrow morning a ten-legged polar bear will appear. Hit it with this magic hammer. Hit it right on top of the head."

The giant handed the boy the hammer. Then they both went to sleep.

Sure enough, early the next morning as the giant snored loudly, the boy sat up and saw a giant ten-legged polar bear. Carrying the hammer, the boy went out to meet the bear. When the boy drew close, the bear reared up. Just as the giant had instructed, the boy scurried around the bear, climbed up its back, and hit it on the top of the head! Immediately the bear rolled on its back. The boy scratched its belly. As the boy walked back to camp, the bear followed him like a frisky pup.

"Now I've adopted a human boy and a ten-legged polar bear," the giant said.

"Well, so be it. Let's have breakfast."

They sat together and ate chunks of whale meat and washed them down with water. As they cleaned up camp, a raven lit down.

"Cawwgggghhh!" the raven said. "Boy, your parents are now paddling their kayak, still searching for you."

"Do they paddle on the river or on the sea?" the boy asked.

"And if they are on the river," the bear said, "do they paddle toward the mouth or away from the mouth?"

"Maybe by now my parents are on the tundra between the river and the sea!" the boy said.

But the raven said no more. It flew off.

The next day, the next, and the next, the three companions traveled south along the seacoast. But they did not find the boy's parents.

They decided to walk inland. They meandered north, south, east, and west, covering as much ground as possible. Sometimes the boy rode on the giant's shoulder. Sometimes the giant set the boy down and told him to wait as he and the ten-legged polar bear traveled in the roundabout way of giants and ten-legged bears. Then they would return to the boy, put what food they had caught on the ground, make camp, eat, and sleep.

"Tomorrow let's go north along the seacoast," the boy said as they got ready to sleep one night.

"All right," the giant said.

They fell asleep. During the night a powerful wind rolled them to the edge of the sea. But they remained asleep. High atop a sea cliff the boy had a dream. In his dream he saw a storm capsize his parents' kayak. His mother and father were flung into the sea and disappeared below the surface.

In the morning the three woke up to find themselves on the very edge of the cliff. Moving back from the cliff, they sat together and ate breakfast. As they ate, a raven swooped in.

"Raven," the boy said, "I am an orphan now. I just know it. A terrible storm capsized my parents' kayak. They were thrown into the sea. They are gone."

"What you say is true," the raven said. "Cawwggghhh! Sadly true, sadly true."

Angered that the bird had refused to tell him where along the seacoast or river his parents might have been found, the boy flung a rock at the raven, knocked it to the ground, and kicked it so hard that it rolled into the sea.

"Sometimes a raven brings bad news," the giant said, "sometimes good."

The boy fell to the ground, wracked with sobs. He cried and cried, and nothing the giant or bear could say solaced him in the least. They were desperate to help but could not. They could only watch as the boy rolled on the ground, crying the way someone cries only when they first are orphaned.

After the boy passed the whole day weeping, a giant loon arrived.

"Boy, I have news for you," the loon said.

The boy stopped crying. "What is it?" he asked.

"Your mother and father now live at the bottom of the sea," the loon said. "I travel back and forth between the Land-of-the-Living and the Land-of-the-Dead, bearing messages. Whenever you have such a message, tell me and I'll deliver it to them."

The boy wept all night.

The next morning the giant began to tap his drum.

"What are you doing?" the boy asked.

"Calling in my wife," the giant said.

Soon the giant's wife arrived. Of course she was a giant as well.

"We must adopt this boy as our own," the giant said to her.

"Well, since we have a big house, of course there's plenty of room for him," she replied. "What about this ten-legged polar bear and this loon?"

"They can live nearby," the giant said.

The giant's wife hoisted the boy up on her shoulder. The two giants, the ten-legged polar bear, the loon, and the boy all set out for the giants' village. By the time they arrived, the boy had fallen asleep. The giant's wife set him down in their house. She tore a piece of her fur collar off and covered the boy with it. The blanket was a perfect fit.

For many years the boy lived in the village of giants. Every day the loon asked, "Is there a message for your mother and father?"

But each time the loon asked, the boy said, "No!" and wept the rest of the day.

Finally the loon said to the boy, "You will always be an orphan, that's true. But you must decide if you want to stop weeping over this. And even if you want to keep on weeping, you could still send your mother and father a message. Think over what I have said."

The boy wept and thought, wept and thought. Another year passed by. The boy was now a young man. He called the loon to his side. "Loon, please bring a message to my parents," he said.

"What shall I tell them?" the loon asked.

"Say that I'm not happy that they are gone," the boy said. "But that I'm happy to be in this village."

"All right," said the loon.

Having heard the boy's request, the loon dove beneath the surface of the sea. The loon swam to the bottom. There he delivered the boy's words to his mother and father.

Soon the loon broke the surface and flew back to the village. "Your parents sent a message in return," the loon said to the boy. "Though they miss you terribly, they are pleased that you are safe in the village of giants."

"What else did they say?" asked the boy.

"Now that you're a young man, they want you to go back to your old village and find a wife," said the loon.

Some days the young man wept. Some days he did not weep. Some days he flung rocks until he knocked a raven from the sky, for it is true that he never lost his anger toward ravens. But soon he took his parents' advice and went back to his old village. He stayed there for a long time. He fell in love and got married. And then he brought his new wife back to the village of giants. They had five children.

The orphan, his wife, and their children often sent messages to the bottom of the sea, and just as often got messages back.

HOW THE NARWHAL GOT
ITS TUSK

THERE WAS A BOY who had been blind since birth. He lived with his mother and father and his aunt, who was his mother's sister. Now, the boy had particularly good hearing, and his parents built their house where the boy could hear both the river and the sea, but behind a gather of wind-break boulders. Ravens and gulls often squalled about begging for scraps of food, and the aunt took special pleasure in scattering them. The aunt kept to one side of the house, and everyone got along just fine, except when the aunt flew into a jealous tantrum.

"You have a fine son and a fine husband," the aunt would say to her sister, "and I don't!" The aunt would tear at her hair, spit, and hiss, her face deeply flushed.

"I can't put up anymore with your jealousy!" the boy's mother would shout. "Sister, get out of here!"

Sobbing wretchedly, the aunt would meander the inlets. She would walk and

walk, mumbling to herself, scattering ravens and gulls alike. Sometimes she would be gone for two or three days. Visiting inlets and scattering ravens and gulls always seemed to calm her down.

Now, one day late in summer, the aunt crouched behind a boulder and watched her nephew sitting with his mother and father near the mouth of the river.

"Beluga whales have come in to feed," the father said. "How many do you suppose are in the mouth of the river now?"

"Six!" the boy shouted. "I hear six whales spouting!"

"Are you sure?" the boy's mother asked.

"Yes, I'm sure," the boy said.

"Well, you are right," the father said.

The boy, his father, and mother loved one another very much. And had the aunt said, "I'll sit with you," they would have welcomed her. Instead, crouched behind a boulder, she got jealous.

"What's that sound I hear coming from behind us?" the boy asked.

"Maybe it's a raven scratching the ground," his mother said. "Or a fox tearing up dry grass with its teeth."

"I'll go look," said the father.

The father snuck up and saw his sister-in-law pulling at her own hair. He saw her chewing on pebbles!

The father returned to his family. "It wasn't a raven and it wasn't a fox," he said.

"It was my sister-in-law. She was yanking at her hair and chewing pebbles. That's what I saw."

Just then, down the beach a ways, the mother and father saw the boy's aunt dragging herself along.

"Is that a wounded seal I hear?" the boy asked.

"I'm afraid it's your aunt," his mother replied.

The aunt got to her feet, flung rocks at her family, then ran until she was out of sight. The boy and his mother and father went home.

The aunt was gone for four days. She wandered every inlet in the territory. She did not eat a bit. She did not sleep. She did not stop to rest, not once, night or day.

Finally the aunt said, "I'm homesick!" But just then she looked out and saw a storm darken the horizon. Now, everyone knows that a storm can rage in very quickly, and that is exactly what this storm was doing. The aunt looked around for shelter, but she did not see any. Suddenly—*whap!*—she was struck by lightning! A crooked tusk of lightning crackled down and hit her!

Back in the house the boy had been whittling a harpoon when he said, "Oh, oh, my aunt has been struck by lightning!" He sometimes blurted out a thing such as this, and it often turned out to be true. "Now the storm has gone out to sea. But my aunt lies sprawled on the beach."

The boy's mother and father ran from the house and went inlet to inlet.

"Look—up ahead!" the mother shouted. "A seal has washed in!"

"That's no seal," the father said. "It's your sister."

They hurried on. What the boy had said was true—his aunt lay stunned on the rocky beach, lightning-singed. They rolled her over. When they heard her moan, they knew that she was still alive. The fur hem of her coat was smoldering. Cupping seawater in their hands, they doused it.

They carried the aunt back to the house. They put blankets over her. They waited. But the aunt did not wake up. She smelled lightning-singed. She moaned.

"Sit next to your aunt," the boy's father said to him. "Here is a bowl of water. If her fur hem or any other part of her clothing flares up, douse it."

It became nighttime. The boy did not leave his aunt's side. The mother and father fell asleep, but the boy stayed awake.

Half the night passed. The boy heard his aunt groan. He touched her hair; it was stiff as feather quills. He touched her forehead; she had a burning fever. He placed a damp cloth on her forehead, lifted the cloth, felt her forehead again; the fever was gone from there. He touched her right elbow—there it was, the fever now resided in her elbow! Her elbow was as hot as a coal. He put the damp cloth on her elbow. He woke up his mother and father.

"Mother, Father—my aunt's fever is traveling about!" the boy cried.

"Yes, that happens sometimes," his mother said. "It happens that a lightning-struck person has a fever that travels. Also, a lightning-struck person gets enormously thirsty. There is no thirst as deep. You have to keep very close watch, because such a person will try and drink seawater, the thirst is that great."

"But for now," the father said, "just give your aunt sips of water."

The mother and father went back to sleep. The boy dripped water from a cloth into his aunt's mouth. To his great delight he heard her swallow, though she was half-asleep. He touched her elbow again—the fever was gone from there. He searched for it and found it in both of her feet.

116   He tore the cloth in half, then swathed his aunt's feet in the damp cloths. He sat

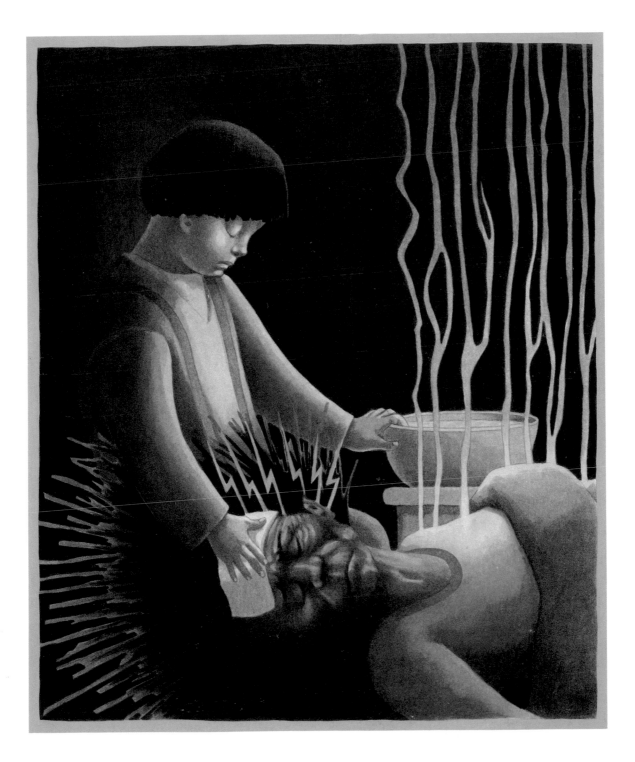

up all night with his aunt. He followed her fever, from feet to knees, from knees to shoulders, and by morning he had bathed her. At dawn he felt his poor aunt's face; she had turned into a craggly old woman.

Finally his aunt sat up awake and said, "It's nice to smell the cooking fire first thing!"

"That's not the cooking fire," the boy said. "It's the sleeves of your coat smoldering. Aunt, you've been lightning-struck." He doused the sleeves.

Though he had not meant them to, the boy's words had terribly upset his aunt. She leapt to her feet, tore the hem and sleeves from her coat, rubbed them in fish oil, and flung them to the ravens and gulls, who carried them off in bits and pieces. Howling with sadness, the aunt fled from the house. The boy called after her, "Aunt! Aunt! Come back!" But his aunt did not turn for home.

When the boy's mother and father awoke, he told them what had happened. They searched every inlet, but the aunt was not to be found. That night no one had much of an appetite, and they all went to bed early. During the night they heard a windstorm howling.

The next morning the boy and his father walked to the mouth of the river. They sat on a low ledge of rock.

"Listen," the father said. "What do you hear?"

The boy tilted his head to the south. "Someone is walking the rocky beach," he

said.

"Yes, it is your aunt," his father said.

"What is she doing?" the boy asked.

"The beach is filled with animals that tumbled in during the storm last night," his father said. "There are a number of seals. Farther down, fish are rotting. Farther yet, a white beluga whale carcass is humped in kelp. Son, anyone but ravens, gulls, and maybe a fox would spit out carrion, but your aunt is having a feast! Oh, oh, oh, she is biting into the whale's tail! This is sad news, but it's true."

"Let's go home and tell my mother," said the boy.

"Yes, we must," his father said.

When they stepped into the house, the boy said, "We found my aunt!"

"Where is she?" asked his mother.

"She's scavenging the rocky beach," her husband said. "She's chewing on a dead whale's tail!"

"This is terrible!" the boy's mother said. "Go fetch my sister! I'll prepare some broth for her."

The boy and his father went back to the beach.

"What's my aunt doing right now?" the boy asked.

"She's taking big gulps of rotting seal flipper," his father said. "You wait here. I'll be right back."

The father ran up and threw sinew-rope around the aunt's legs, tripped her, and carried her up to the boy.

"I have your aunt over my shoulder now," the father said. "Let's go home."

The aunt was kicking and shouting, "Let me go! Let me go!" The boy followed this sound.

When they got back inside, the aunt fell right to sleep. She slept the rest of the afternoon. At suppertime the aunt was still sleeping. "What can we do about my aunt?" the boy asked. He was quite worried.

"Lightning-struck people are unpredictable," his father said.

"Yes," said his mother. "All we can do is offer her broth and douse any part of her clothing that flares up."

"That's about all we can do," the father said.

"I smell winter in the air," said the boy.

"Yes, the edges of the river are icing up," his father said. "And soon the sea will freeze over."

The boy, his mother, and father fell asleep. But in the middle of the night, the aunt startled awake. The boy heard his aunt, but pretended to be asleep. The aunt muttered, gnawed at her collar, muttered, muttered, tossed, and turned.

This must be my aunt's restlessness, the boy thought, *the kind that inhabits a person just before winter sets in.*

But then he heard his aunt get to her feet, open the door, and walk out. He waited a short while, then followed her. He heard his aunt up ahead. She was walking toward the mouth of the river. It was snowing. Snow crunched underfoot. His aunt stayed close to the river. The boy picked his way along, using the harpoon he had been whittling as a walking stick.

They walked until morning, to the mouth of the river, then along the beach, back to the river, and then south along the riverbank. Finally the boy's aunt sat down to rest. A little upriver the boy sat down, too. It snowed and snowed, and then a full-blown blizzard swirled in. The sea had frozen and icy winds skidded off the ice and whipped the boy's face. "Aunt! Aunt! Aunt! Are you there?"

Nearly as blind as her nephew in the blizzard, the aunt still managed to find him. She felt sorry for him. But she was angry, too.

Shaking her nephew by the shoulders, she said, "Why have you followed me?"

"To bring you back home," the boy sobbed. "There's broth, a good fire, freshly caught fish, I'm sure."

"Nephew, stop trying to help me," the aunt said. "I've been lightning-struck. I've become an eater of rotten seal flippers, fish eyes, and bird throats. This is bad luck. Bad luck. What's more, I'm more thirsty than you can possibly imagine. Oh, oh, oh. I had a good plan. I was going to walk until freeze-up. Then I'd find a seal breathing hole, chisel it wider, slip through, and drink water to my satisfaction. But now I have you with me, nephew. I must take care of you until spring."

"How far are we from the village?" the boy asked.

"Very far," the aunt said. "Too far for your parents to find you; besides, they don't know in which direction to even begin looking. What's more, it is the time of blizzards, too. It would be foolish of you to set out for home now. I'll build an igloo. I have a seal-oil lamp with me. We'll stay together until ice-breakup. Then I'll point you in the direction home. And I'll leap into the sea."

Stepping out on the river ice, the aunt used the boy's harpoon to carve out igloo pieces. She built an igloo, lit the seal-oil lamp inside, and huddled with her nephew.

Day after day, blizzards kept on battering the igloo. There was little food, only a few morsels the boy had brought and a rotten fish his aunt had kept under her coat. One day a ptarmigan wandered into the igloo and immediately the aunt fell on it. She cooked half and gave it to the boy. The other half she let rot, then ate it herself.

The boy had brought along his knife and kept busy whittling the harpoon. By expert touch he whittled in the faces of seals, birds, whales all down its length. Near the bottom of the harpoon, he whittled in the faces of his mother, his father, and his own face, all of which he knew from touch.

"Why did you not whittle my face into the harpoon?" the aunt asked.

"Why, Aunt, I'm eventually going to give you this harpoon," the boy said. "And you will be able to see the faces of your family whenever you want."

All the rest of the winter, the two survived on freshly caught fish; the aunt let her share get rotten before she ate. Now and then a ptarmigan happened into the igloo as well. The aunt was very restless and paced back and forth, back and forth. "It is strange to sit out the winter with a lightning-struck aunt," the boy said.

"It's your fault," the aunt said. "You shouldn't have followed me."

Back and forth the aunt paced, back and forth, until one day the boy said, "I hear the ice-breakup!" and the aunt rushed outside to look.

"Yes, it's finally spring," the aunt said.

"Let's walk to the edge of the sea," the boy said.

At the edge of the sea, they sat and listened to the thundering ice-breakup.

Suddenly the aunt cried out, "I know I said I'd point you in the direction home before I leapt into the sea, but I can't wait!" She brushed by her nephew and flung herself into the sea!

Now all along the boy had been wearing a sinew-rope as a belt. He quickly fastened the rope to his harpoon. He listened hard. He heard his aunt flailing about in the sea. He flung his harpoon. He had hoped that the harpoon would slap down near his aunt, so that she might grab it and he could pull her to safety. Instead, the harpoon pierced his aunt directly through the upper lip. Thrashing about wildly, his aunt cried out, "Nephew, you have struck me with the harpoon!"

Panic and remorse gathered in the boy's heart. He stood helplessly at the water's edge. "Aunt!" he called. "Where are you?"

His aunt rolled in on a wave, grabbed the boy by his ankles, and dragged him into the sea!

Quite far out the aunt took her nephew below the surface. The boy was all but certain he would drown. But then his aunt began to swim them upward.

At that moment—just then—from the spin of things, the whirlpool caused by his aunt's swirling upward, the boy felt his aunt's hair braiding tightly around the harpoon, fixing it to her mouth—a long, spiral, extended tooth! Then they burst into the air and gasped with a sound as loud as two whales spouting. And then his aunt simply let the boy go free and sank away.

Still gasping for breath—for he could hardly swim at all—the boy thrashed toward the sound of ravens on the beach. Finally he managed to drag himself up onto the beach. He sparked two rocks together and made a fire, dried out his clothes, put them back on, and sat a long time by the fire, thinking about his aunt.

In a while he stood near the sea again. He listened. He heard scraping and clacking. It was a sound that he had never heard before.

"What is that?" he asked. "Who is making such a sound?"

"It is I—your aunt!" a voice said.

"What are you doing?" the boy asked.

"I am sharpening my tusk on the rocks," his aunt said. "Lean down and touch what shape I am."

The boy reached out. He touched his aunt. He discovered that his aunt was now a whale!

124   "Yes," his aunt said, "I have become a whale. I am the kind called a narwhal. I am

the first of my kind to have this long tusk, but from now on all of us will have it. I am the only one who will have seal, bird, whale, and human faces carved into its tusk, though."

"You mean, my harpoon became your tusk?" the boy asked.

"That is right," his aunt said.

"Do you drink from the sea?" the boy asked.

"Yes," the aunt replied.

"I must tell my mother and father what has happened to you," the boy said. "They will have been worrying all winter."

"First, leap onto my back," said the aunt.

Without question the boy slid down the rocks and climbed onto his aunt's back. She took him out to sea. She dove to the bottom. To his great surprise, the boy could breathe underwater. At the bottom his whale-aunt rubbed kelp, seaweed, and other sea vines over her nephew's eyelids. They stung him harshly. Then his aunt lifted him to the surface and set him back on the rocks.

"Start off for home," his aunt said. "I have rubbed your eyes in a sea-broth that cures blindness. By the time you get home, you'll know that I have told the truth."

"Let's stay and talk awhile," the boy said. "It is strange to be leaning out from rocks, talking to my aunt who has become a narwhal."

"No," said his aunt. "I must dive down again. It's time for the spring lightning storms. Lightning may be looking for me right now! I must go."

"Good-bye, then, Aunt," the boy said.

"Good-bye, Nephew," his aunt said. She disappeared deep into the sea. Suddenly he heard a loud crackling sound out over the sea, and he turned to it. And he saw a crooked tusk of lightning flash through the distant storm clouds! He *saw* it!

Next he saw ravens, then seagulls.

He hurried home.

At home he saw the faces of his mother and father.

He told them everything that had happened. They ate supper together. They talked and laughed, and then his mother and father fell asleep. But the boy stayed awake all night, looking at their faces.

THE GIRL WHO
DREAMED ONLY GEESE

A LONG TIME AGO a girl lived with her mother and father in a village near the marshes. She was ten. All through her childhood she heard about how her ancestors were great, proud geese-dreamers. Her own mother and father dreamed only about geese. No, they did not dream about anything else, just geese. Then, in the spring of her tenth year, a terrible thing happened. Her mother and father stopped dreaming geese. There had been no warning of this; they just stopped.

This disturbed everyone in the village. "It's a great privilege to dream geese," a man said to her parents. "Besides, you know full well that if you don't dream about them, the geese will be insulted and might not fly north to our marshes."

"We no longer care," the girl's father said.

"Geese chased by foxes. Geese squabbling. Geese shedding their feathers. Geese laying eggs. Geese honking in the sky. Geese, geese, geese, geese, geese," the girl's mother said. "We are sick and tired of doing the work of geese-dreaming!"

"Yes," said the girl's father, "we are leaving the geese-dreaming up to our daughter now. She's old enough."

"You have many years of geese-dreaming left," another village man said. "You are being selfish. I think you should be sent off to live by yourselves at the edge of the marshes!"

"We agree!" the other villagers shouted.

"Very well," the girl's parents said, then they left the village and made camp at the edge of the marshes. The girl stayed behind in her old house.

Much to everyone's happiness, the girl proved to be good at dreaming geese. That very spring the flocks arrived; hunters went out and came back with armfuls of geese. They killed only what they needed, for there were fish, ducks, ptarmigan, and other animals to eat as well. There was much joy, because once again the marshes were loud with geese. It was a good summer. And at the end of summer the flocks went south.

The girl dreamed geese for three years. Everyone was pleased. The villagers, in a forgiving mood, were just about to ask the girl's parents back to the village. But in the spring of her thirteenth year, the girl's luck took a turn for the worse—night after night she dreamed a sky empty of geese!

Early one morning a powerful shaman came to visit. He had heard about the girl's powers to dream geese, and he was jealous. In front of a lot of villagers, the shaman said to the girl, "What did you dream last night?"

"No geese in front of the moon," the girl answered. "No geese in the sky at all!"

"This village is in deep trouble," the shaman said.

"Keep trying to dream geese!" a woman pleaded with the girl.

That night the girl tried sleeping in different places in her house. She tried sleeping outside on the ground. No luck.

It got to be summer. Out by the marshes the girl's mother said, "The geese have never been this late!"

"You're right," her husband replied.

All along the girl had not dreamed geese. One morning the shaman demanded of the girl, "Tell me, what did you dream last night?"

"No geese," the girl said, weeping.

Hearing this, the shaman went to every house, gathering the villagers together. "Now," he said to the girl, "tell us what you dreamed last night."

"An empty sky," said the girl. "No geese at all in it."

"Hasn't it been long enough for you to see that the girl's head is empty of geese?" the shaman asked everyone.

The eldest woman in the village stepped forth. "A summer without geese," she said. "That means the world is upside down. Bad luck. Bad luck. Without geese in the marshes, life is no longer familiar. I might as well lie down and die."

The old woman threw herself to the ground and clawed at the dirt.

"It's all my fault," said the girl.

"You need a new geese-dreamer around here!" the shaman said.

"Who but someone in the girl's family can dream geese properly?" a man said.

"Me!" said the shaman. "I'll dream in the geese."

Now everyone turned to see the girl's parents standing at the edge of the village. "No—wait!" the girl's mother said. "Give our daughter one more chance!"

It was agreed that the girl would have another night to try to dream geese down to the marshes.

In the morning the villagers stood next to her. The girl woke up. The eldest woman said, "What did you dream?"

"One goose!" the girl said.

"A goose! A goose! A goose!" the villagers shouted.

The girl looked up. "Mother, Father, you must paddle out and catch that goose."

Her mother and father quickly climbed into their skin-boat and paddled out on the marshes.

"Go back to your houses," the girl told the villagers. "Put on your best clothes. Get ready for a feast."

The villagers were longing to savor the taste of even one wild goose; they went into their houses. The shaman stayed with the girl.

When everyone was out of sight, the girl threw herself to the ground. "One goose," she cried. "I could dream only *one*. I'm causing such misery. I'm causing such disappointment. I may even cause the eldest woman to die. I'm a curse on my family. I'm a curse on my village."

"I'm afraid all of what you say is true," the shaman said.

"What can I do?" the girl asked.

"You must go away," the shaman said. "For the good of your village. For the good of your family. You must go across the plain, in the opposite direction of the marshes. Keep walking until you reach the outskirts of the world. There, build a hermit's hut and live alone for the rest of your days."

"But out on that plain lives the Thrashing Spirit," the girl said. "I shiver to think of that monster, who thrashes people to death."

"I'll use my powers to see that the Thrashing Spirit doesn't harm you," the shaman said.

"If I go away, will you dream in the flocks?" said the girl.

"The way it'll be," said the shaman, "is I'll do the geese-dreaming from now on. The way it'll be is as soon as you build your hermit's hut, I'll dream in the flocks. The marshes will be loud with geese. There'll be plenty to eat."

"Very well then," the girl said.

Quickly, before her mother and father returned, the girl packed a bundle of food and set out in the direction opposite the marshes.

She walked and walked. Far from the village she looked back. She wept. She walked and walked until she disappeared below the horizon.

Finally her mother and father ran back into the village, where all the people waited. The father held a goose by its neck. "Look, daughter, I caught the goose!" he shouted.

"Daughter, daughter," the girl's mother said. "Come share our luck."

They searched everywhere but could not find their daughter.

"Give me that goose," the shaman said, grabbing the goose from the father's hands. The shaman worked some magic, then held out the goose for everyone to see that it was now just a goose decoy made of twigs! The shaman quickly built a fire and tossed the decoy into it. Soon it crackled. "That girl could only dream in a twig-goose!" the shaman said.

"Where's our daughter?" the girl's mother asked.

"She knew that she was causing bad luck around here," said the shaman. "I convinced her to leave—we can't have a girl whose head is empty of geese doing the geese-dreaming for us, now, can we?"

Hearing this, the girl's mother and father leapt on the shaman, beating him with their fists, tearing out handfuls of his hair. Some villagers pulled them apart.

"Keep them away from me," the shaman said, and the villagers obeyed. They took the girl's parents back to their camp at the edge of the marshes.

"Tonight," said the shaman, "I'll dream geese."

That night the shaman slept in the girl's house. In the morning when he woke up, the villagers gathered near him.

"What did you dream?" the eldest woman asked.

But before he could answer, some hunters hurried in and right away they kicked the shaman. "No geese," one hunter said. "No geese out there in the marshes. No geese. None at all."

"I *did* dream geese!" the shaman cried. "But—ah—um—in my dream, my geese got all confused and forgot which way *north* was!"

But the villagers did not believe him. They swatted him with dog harnesses.

"No, no—hear me out!" the shaman said. "What happened was—ah—um—my geese got blinded by the moon. Yes, that's it. Now my geese are wandering around lost in the sky."

Again the villagers thought the shaman was lying. They hollered directly into his ears, "Honk, honk, honk, honk, honk, honk," until he could not take it any longer and crawled from the village. That night the shaman slept between the village and the marshes.

Back in their camp the girl's parents tossed and turned in terrible sleep and finally woke up at the same time. "I dreamed that our daughter had filthy braids," the mother said.

"I dreamed the same thing," the father said.

"In your dream," said the mother, "where was our daughter sitting?"

"At the outskirts of the world," the father said.

Immediately they got dressed, packed bundles of food, and set out in the direction opposite the marshes. They walked all through the night. They walked all morning. They were far from the marshes, far from the village.

Finally they stopped to rest. They looked around. Up ahead they saw a horrible sight. A Thrashing Spirit was moving quickly along the ground toward them.

"Nobody has ever survived a Thrashing Spirit," the father said. "Let's turn back."

"Our daughter is at the outskirts of the world," the mother said. "Tell me, husband, do you want to see her again? Tell me, do you want to see the great flocks again? Tell me, do you want life to be familiar again?"

The father stepped forth to meet the Thrashing Spirit. He held his harpoon high at the ready. The mother had a length of strongly plaited fishing line ready as well. The Thrashing Spirit drew close. It was loud. It was so ugly, they could barely look at it. Still, they kept a close watch, because a Thrashing Spirit could get around behind and thrash them. It was a standoff. Finally the Thrashing Spirit attacked. It thrashed at the man and woman. But they moved safely off to one side. Then the father threw his harpoon, piercing the Thrashing Spirit deep down to its bones. It fell thudding to the ground, wailing and thrashing about, but it did not die. So the mother choked it with the fishing line. Both things were necessary. The Thrashing Spirit was very powerful. But now it was dead.

"Let's not sit around by a dead Thrashing Spirit," the mother said.

"Let's set out toward our daughter," the father said.

They traveled for three more days. Early on the fourth morning, they saw a hut up ahead. They hurried to the hut. When they first saw their daughter, she lay on the ground, her filthy braids stiff, her clothes shabby and torn, her eyes rolled back in her head. What's more, her body was crusted all over with dirt. When her mother reached out and touched her arm, the girl suddenly hissed and clawed at both her parents, spit, scowled, bared her teeth. Her teeth chattered, she shivered fiercely, then fainted—just blacked out.

The girl was so thin and weak, her parents thought that she might die. They put a few drops of water on her lips and she came to. Her mother then prepared some broth and fed it to her a little at a time. The mother and father bathed their daughter clean. Slowly, day after day, she regained some strength. But she was still quite ill. She could hardly move her arms or legs. More days went by, and now she could at least recognize her mother and father. Finally she could take a few steps.

Much of the summer went by. One morning the girl said her first words in all of this time. "The shaman was jealous of me," she said. "He caused my head to be empty of geese. He never wanted our village to have geese. And so he has trapped the flocks on the moon. From out here, at the outskirts of the world, I saw him do this."

"Are you strong enough to travel?" asked the girl's mother.

"Yes," she answered.

They all set out for the village. They would tell the villagers what evil the shaman had done. Because the girl was still a little weak, the journey took them ten days. When they arrived, they saw that the villagers had not starved. There were ducks, ptarmigan, and fish to eat. Yet they did not see the eldest woman of the village.

"Where's the eldest one?" the girl asked.

Suddenly, from the edge of the village, the shaman said, "She lay down and died."

The girl turned to the shaman. "You lied about being able to dream in geese. You

have many powers, but not the power to dream geese!" she said with anger. "You have hoarded the geese for yourself on the moon! You can fly up there. You will have plenty of geese to eat, and there will be none for us."

The girl's father hit the shaman on the head with a cooking pot, then dragged him to the center of the village. The father knew how to tie knots that would keep even a shaman from working loose for a while; he did that.

They all waited for darkness, and when it came, everyone looked up at the moon. There they saw the shadows of the geese, flying every which way, yet unable to break from the territory of the moon.

"The girl was right," said a villager, "the shaman trapped the flocks on the moon!"

The girl said, "I'm going to sleep now. I will try to dream geese down from the moon." She lay down on the ground, right then and there. The rest of the villagers went into their houses, but the girl's mother and father sat with her.

The shaman was left in the middle of the village. The knots were working well so far.

First thing in the morning, hunters paddled out on the marshes and came home with armfuls of geese.

Late into morning the moon could still be seen in the sky. Geese poured down from the moon, all morning, all day. All day geese arrived to the marshes.

That night there was a great feast and much rejoicing. The geese had quieted down in the marshes, but the villagers knew that geese were out there.

During the night the shaman worked loose from the ropes and fled to the moon, now empty of geese. He hid there a long time.

Life was familiar again. From that day forward, the girl dreamed geese very often. And dreamed only geese, nothing else. Geese chased by foxes. Geese squabbling. Geese honking. Geese flying north. Geese flying south. The girl lived to be very, very old, she who did the geese-dreaming work in her village, and she was greatly respected.

Here the story ends.

STORY NOTES

THE DAY PUFFINS NETTED HID-WELL

This Labrador-Inuit story is the result of a two-year correspondence with linguist-zoologist Peter Stolper. He sent me eight versions of the story and fragments of two other versions. In Labrador, Canada, he had worked with a man named William Etajuak, who died in 1983. Peter Stolper and I exchanged about sixty letters concerning "The Day Puffins Netted Hid-Well," and through these letters we worked to complete the story. Many of the letters had copies of Etajuak's own drawings of bird nests, canoes, hunting and fishing maps of the Labrador coast, and even a makeshift Labrador-Inuit cookbook. Peter Stolper wrote: "In Etajuak's tale, sometimes villagers hunt auks, sometimes puffins. Always, though, the relationship between father and son is crucial. This is a family story."

NOAH AND THE WOOLLY MAMMOTHS

Though Mark Nuqac told his Noah stories between 1977 and 1980, the cautious behavior of the villagers as they first approach the ark perhaps represents the Inuit people's tense curiosity and vigilance when they first saw white people arrive in their tall-masted schooners centuries ago. Mark Nuqac had a propensity for recasting any number of Biblical stories from his own point of view. In "A Moses Story" (as he called it), instead of having Moses cross a scorching desert and confront a burning bush, he has Moses stumble and meander over the tundra. Moses engages in mortal combat with several menacing spirit figures and has an oracular "vision" of Sedna, the great Inuit Goddess-of-the-Sea, who is about to punish a village of Inuit for breaking her strict rules about greed and lying. Later in the tale, Sedna sends forth a "plague" of spear-tusked walrus, which roil the waters for days, capsizing kayaks and drowning fleeing Inuit men, women, children, and sled dogs that are whirled to the bottom of the sea.

WHY THE RUDE VISITOR WAS FLUNG BY WALRUS

This story was told by Moses Nuqac, Mark Nuqac's uncle. He was a prolific and boisterous raconteur, and it was easy to see how much he loved spinning tales about shamans. Throughout the North, shamans are notorious, hypnotic, mysterious, and powerful figures. Shamans are capable of great evil; they are likewise capable of heroic deeds. A doctor-shaman may deftly cure a patient's fever, but he may curse an enemy with mental dilapidation, nightmares, or broken bones. A shaman may fly to the moon or dive down to the Land-of-the-Dead. A shaman may levitate a flotilla of walrus, throw a tantrum in the form of an ice storm, or dream a good-luck name for a newborn child. A shaman can communicate with the spirit world. Needless to say, then, a shaman's behavior is often quite dramatic. When a shaman shows up in a village, there is seldom a dull moment. Often in Moses Nuqac's stories, a shaman purposely stirs up trouble. Day-to-day village life suddenly seems unfamiliar, and there's a lot of fear and anxiety. Yet finally the villagers muster their communal strength; relying on their boldest thoughts and actions, they ultimately defeat the intruder. Life once again becomes familiar.

In my notebooks I recorded eleven of Moses Nuqac's tales in which a particularly grisly, cantankerous, slovenly, bragging shaman wears an astonishingly smelly shirt. This shaman, whose name is Tiuk, often sends his reeking sidekick shirt on ahead to announce his impending arrival. Though the Inuit villagers in these stories are accustomed to shamans utilizing inanimate objects—sleds, harnesses, shoes, driftwood—for their own purposes, they have never before experienced something quite so puzzling and repulsive as a shirt that smells like a thousand rotting whale carcasses! All in all, Moses Nuqac's shaman stories are some of the most inventive, hilarious, and vivid I have ever heard.

UTERITSOQ AND THE DUCKBILL DOLLS

This story derives from three tape-recorded renditions by Jack Umik, a Greenlandic Inuit man. They were told to linguist Helen Tanizaki, who prepared the working draft on which I based my retelling. A story entitled "Uteritsoq, the Obstinate One," which contains similar incidents and themes, was published in 1939 in Knud Rasmussen's *Posthumous Notes on East Greenland Legends and Myths* (edited by Hother B. S. Ostermann). In that earlier incarnation, the story makes no mention of duckbill dolls, or as Jack Umik also sometimes called them, "orphan dolls." Perhaps Jack Umik invented the dolls. Or perhaps he heard about them in another tale and borrowed them; motifs, incidents, even specific passages of dialogue are shared between storytellers. What is most important is that a story, for all of its changes or its reluctance to change, survives by being *told,* generation after generation.

THE WOLVERINE'S SECRET

This story is based on two recorded versions of an Inuit story from the Mackenzie Delta, brought to me by folklorist David Todd. I have always been particularly fond of Inuit stories that feature wolverines, whose incessant wandering, inventive troublemaking, spiritual power, and physical stamina are celebrated and feared. Another Mackenzie Delta story chronicles a wolverine's adventures during a single night; the animal walks and walks and walks, until it has "exhausted the moon." Then the dawn arrives.

THE GIRL WHO WATCHED IN THE NIGHTTIME

This story is based on nine variations recorded by I'osif Serkin, a Russian linguist. Again, in the literature, an older version exists; it was told by an elder named Nipe'wgi in the Siberian village of Uni'sak and was translated in 1913 by Waldemar Bogoras in *The Eskimo of Siberia*. In 1921 another linguist, Caryn Lister, wrote, "Kidnapping is a common, and particularly onerous, phenomenon in many Siberian folktales. I have collected stories in which fox kidnap children, men kidnap children, even magical parts of the forest kidnap children."

HOW THE NARWHAL GOT ITS TUSK

This origin story, in which the transformation of a lightning-struck woman into a tusked narwhal gives her a shaman's power to heal her nephew's blindness, was originally told by a Greenlandic Inuit man named Pioopiula to Severance and Michael Rosegood, both musicologists and linguists. In their Toronto apartment, I worked with the Rosegoods over a three-week period, listening again and again to the tape recordings they had made, trying to catch the nuances of voice and cadence, the lulls and crescendos in Pioopiula's telling. With Pioopiula's consent, we later added several sentences from versions of the same story told by other Greenlandic storytellers, all recorded by Severance Rosegood. The Rosegoods discussed our final version with Pioopiula, who approved. Before he died in 1986, Pioopiula carried on the vital tradition of telling stories about the origins of life in the Arctic, the first spirit-beings, the appearance of the Inuit, their invention of snowshoes and dogsleds, the first contact with white people, and so on. "He was a true historian," Severance Rosegood wrote in a letter. "His stories about the origins of weather, certain animals, and landforms were, I think, particular favorites."

THE MAN WHO MARRIED A SEAGULL, HOME AMONG THE GIANTS, *and* THE GIRL WHO DREAMED ONLY GEESE

As stated in the introduction, these stories were told by Billy Nuuq, in both Churchill and Eskimo Point. After our initial work together in the North, he moved to a hospital and rest home in Montreal and we exchanged a few letters concerning the stories. He was emphatic about keeping certain aspects of his tales sharp and clear and untampered with. For example, of his story "The Girl Who Dreamed Only Geese," which covers a great deal of time and geographical distance, and involves several epic journeys, he said that when his own grandfather told this story, once the Thrashing Spirit had been killed, it turned "into the daughter." One could determine, then, that in this older version, the girl banished by the shaman to live out her days in remote exile had become a predatory spirit; her own parents kill her, and she is released back into her human form. Yet Billy insisted (in a letter and in person) that, in his rendition, I "leave the [Thrashing Spirit] out there to rot," and that the parents forge on to discover and heal their daughter. Wild and disheveled as she is, she survived *as a human*. Both versions offer powerful examples of the human spirit's will to survive.

ABOUT THE AUTHOR

HOWARD NORMAN is an award-winning author of fiction and a respected translator of folklore. His first novel, *The Northern Lights,* published in 1987, won a Mrs. Giles Whiting Writers Award and was a finalist for the National Book Award. Seven years later his second novel, *The Bird Artist,* was also a finalist for the National Book Award. He has spent considerable time in the Arctic and the Northwest Territories of Canada, researching and writing documentary and ethnographic films and articles about natural history. Long interested in recording the rich legacy of storytelling in the North, he has written several previous collections, including *Northern Tales: Traditional Stories of Eskimo and Indian Peoples*, part of the Pantheon Folklore and Fairy Tale Library. Recipient of a Guggenheim Fellowship and a Lannan Literary Award for Fiction, Mr. Norman is a professor of English at the University of Maryland, and divides his time between Washington, D.C., and Vermont.

ABOUT THE ILLUSTRATORS

LEO & DIANE DILLON have illustrated more than twenty-five books together. Awarded the Caldecott Medal in 1976 for *Why Mosquitoes Buzz in People's Ears,* retold by Verna Aardema, and again in 1977 for *Ashanti to Zulu: African Traditions* by Margaret Musgrove, they have continued to receive numerous awards for their exceptional work, including a Coretta Scott King Award, a *Boston Globe–Horn Book* Award, and three *New York Times* Best Illustrated Awards. The Dillons live and work in Brooklyn, New York.

The color art in this book was done with acrylics on hot-press watercolor board.
The black-and-white friezes were inspired by the stonecut art of the Inuit people
and were done with tempera and ink on scratchboard with the assistance of Lee Dillon.
The display type was set in Weiss Initials Series 2 by Solotype, Oakland, California.
The text type was set in Meridien by Thompson Type, San Diego, California.
Color separations by Bright Arts, Ltd., Singapore
Printed and bound by Tien Wah Press, Singapore
This book was printed on totally chlorine-free Nymolla Matte Art paper.
Production supervision by Stanley Redfern and Ginger Boyer
Designed by Kaelin Chappell and Leo & Diane Dillon